MIDLIFE BABY

A LATER IN LIFE BABY ROMANCE

PIPER SULLIVAN

Copyright © 2019 by Piper Sullivan

All rights reserved.

No part of this book may be reproduced in any form or by any electronic or mechanical means, including information storage and retrieval systems, without written permission from the author, except for the use of brief quotations in a book review.

ENJOY SPICY ROMANCES?

Download Safeguarded for FREE Now!

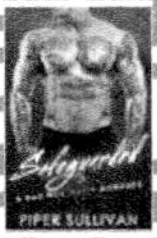
PIPER SULLIVAN

CHAPTER 1
MARGOT

~M^{ay}

"Anything else?"

Grady was an imposing figure as he stood on the other side of the bar, tattooed arms folded over his massive chest, blue eyes glaring down at me with disdain.

I wasn't in the mood to spar with him, not today. Not after the news I'd just gotten from my ex, Michael. I glared up at Grady with the exact disdain he'd shown me, and raised my mostly full martini glass. "Have I asked for anything else? Does it look like my glass is empty, or close to empty Grady?"

He sucked in a breath and clenched his jaw, before he

exhaled slowly, as if physically reaching out in search of patience. "Fine." That was it, all he said to me before he turned and walked away without so much as a look back.

I sighed and turned back to my drink. It was a good martini. The perfect ratio of gin to vermouth, with just a splash of olive brine. Grady, for all his flaws, made a perfect martini, which of course I would never admit to him. But I *would* tip him accordingly.

"Happy Birthday!"

The roar from the big booth in the corner drew my attention, and then my annoyance. Nina, the chef at Dark Horse, was there with the restaurant manager Devon and his new boyfriend, as well as a few other members of the waitstaff. They were all smiles as they celebrated someone's birthday, but all I could see was Devon's grin as he pressed a kiss to his lover's lips. That small move frustrated me, because it reminded me of my own ex-husband Michael and his new husband. And the happily ever after they'd gained at my expense.

I turned away and waved in Grady's direction, but he was too busy flirting with a group of professional women enjoying after work drinks to notice. I sighed and let my shoulders fall in disappointment. Why should a slight by a bartender bother me, when my ex-husband is getting the life we should have had together? *Why?* I snorted in response to my silently asked question, the answer was the one common denominator here.

It was me. *I* was the problem.

Nina sidled up to the bar and smacked both hands on the counter, her wide smile aimed at Grady, who actually looked up at her with a toothy grin and a sparkle in his eyes.

"Barkeep!"

Grady laughed, finished up with the women and walked to the other end of the bar. He stopped in front of Nina, still giving me the cold shoulder. "What'll it be Chef?"

Nina's eyes widened in surprise. "Only my employees call me Chef, does that mean you work for me now?"

Grady's lips twitched, and I had to bite back a moan at the sight of those thick, pale pink lips fighting not to laugh. "Maybe I just forgot your name?"

She laughed. "Now I know you're full of it. I'm unforgettable."

"Yeah, I guess," he conceded and folded his arms, the picture of patience while he waited for her to order.

Nina sighed. "You really are a brick wall sometimes." She shook her head, a genuine smile still fixed on her face. "I'll have two shots of tequila, top shelf, a dark draft, and two margaritas. Please *and* thank you."

Grady was already pouring the shots and filling an icy mug with a dark liquid as he gave Nina the total. "Frozen, or rocks margaritas?"

She glanced over her shoulder at the table where Devon cuddled with his boyfriend and turned back with a sigh. "They strike me as rocks guys, so let's go with that."

Grady nodded and poured several different liquids into a silver cocktail shaker, and I could admit, to myself, that it was truly impressive that he could just whip up what customers wanted without consulting a recipe book or website. He rimmed two glasses with salt and set all the glasses onto a tray.

"Need some help?"

"Nah, I was a waitress all through culinary school. But first," she smiled and lifted the shot glasses off the tray, and slid one towards Grady.

I groaned and rolled my eyes at her blatant flirting, which earned me a glare from them both.

"Anyway," Nina said and lifted her glass in the air. "To the birthday boy. Let's hope the next trip around the sun is as good, *or better*, than the last one. Happy Birthday." She knocked her glass back drained it before slamming the glass on the wooden bar with a satisfied sigh.

"Thanks." Grady knocked the shot back with a smile so sexy that I pinched my knees together.

Nina shrugged and sauntered off, making me wonder if the woman had actually been flirting with the handsome bartender, or if she was just that cheerful. They were friendly, but that seemed to be all it was, which meant I'd just given the temperamental chef another reason to dislike me.

"Great." One little comment about how she'd be much prettier with a normal hair color, and since then she'd been borderline civil to me, and usually only when Pippa or Ryan were around to see it.

"Problem?" Grady turned to me and his smile promptly slipped, which really was a shame, because he was handsome on a good day, but he was the kind of man who only looked better when he smiled, when he let go of that masculine façade and let his emotions show. He wasn't my type of course, but I was a flesh and blood woman who could appreciate what a fine physical specimen he was. Even the bald head worked with his crisp blue eyes and thick red beard. The tight white t-shirt stretched across his massive chest only finished off the look of a slightly bored bartender who knew he was hot stuff.

"No problem, no," I grumble annoyed at him, or myself. I couldn't tell anymore. "Happy birthday. It's my birthday too."

"Happy birthday," he said with as little emotion as he could muster and walked away. Again. I shouldn't be disappointed, not when I was the reason things were the way they were between us, but I was. It was good for me, and probably for him, that we maintained a healthy distance fueled by general dislike. A guy like Grady was fifteen shades of trouble, and none of them were my color. He was trouble in tight-fitting jeans and I wasn't in the market for trouble. Never had been.

Despite all that, I wished he would smile at me the way he smiled at every other woman in town. But he wouldn't, I'd made sure of it, so I sucked down my lukewarm margarita and ordered another. And then another.

As the hours passed, my sullen drunkenness turned into a melancholy tipsy-ness that warmed me and made me forget—a little—about Michael and his happiness. Not that he didn't deserve it, he did more than just about anyone I knew, but the way he'd gotten it was what I had a hard time accepting.

A shadow fell over me and blocked out the lighting fixture above my bar seat. "Ready to pay up," Grady growled, even sterner than usual.

I looked up with a frown. "Kicking me out so soon?"

Grady did something unexpected, he laughed. "Not quite." He motioned towards the rest of the bar, and when I followed his line of sight I saw that the place was empty. When I turned back to him, he wore a smile that lacked any warmth or amusement. "Contrary to what you think of me Margot, I know how to treat my customers. Even the bitchy ones."

"I deserve that," I conceded, because what else could I do? "But I actually don't think you're a bad businessman."

He snorted. "It's just my particular *unseemly* bar that you have a problem with."

I shook my head as he threw my own word back at me. "That was about a particular event, not your entire business. This place is perfect for many of the events Carlotta has booked here, but not a superstar bachelor party."

"Right." He produced a rag and wiped down the bar.

"You're the last one standing, so are you ready to pay? Because the bar is officially closed."

"I'm ready," I told him and finished the last swig of martini. It was time to get out of here and far away from him. I reached for my favorite glittery red clutch to pay the tab, and the purse slid off the bar and to the floor, it's contents scattering everywhere. "Oops," I giggled to myself and reached for the purse again, only to find myself sprawled on the floor right beside the clutch. "Whoa! Slippery stool," I laughed nervously, aware of a watchful pair of blue eyes focused on my every move as I tried—and failed—to get to my feet. "Dammit!"

CHAPTER 2
GRADY

She was sloshed.

Completely and totally wasted. Margot Devereaux-Blanchard was drunk off her ass. And adorable, blast the annoying woman. The last thing I needed to be reminded of was my own inconvenient attraction to the stuck up harpy. She went out of her way to let me know I wasn't in her league, that my business was below her standards, to show her disdain for me, but watching her spread out on my bar floor giggling, none of it mattered. I hopped over the bar and squatted down to help Margot to her feet.

"Did you eat anything with those martinis?"

She grunted as she tried to stand, her ridiculous red stiletto slipped and she was on the ground again.

"I'll take that as a no."

"You only serve greasy bar food, and I don't eat greasy

food in a bar, or otherwise," she answered haughtily. It wasn't a surprise she didn't eat fatty foods, her body told the story. She was of average height and perfectly lean except in her tits and her hips, especially in the navy blue dress she wore. Her silver hair was pinned up to show off sharp cheekbones, a delicate jaw and a slender neck. Her violet eyes missed nothing and expressed everything, even what she wished to hide her emotions. Her stomach growled, and she covered it as if that could hide the noise.

I laughed at her. Even tipsy and wobbly on her heels, she could manage to get in a snobby jab. "Sorry to tell you honey, but a salad ain't gonna sober you up."

My words had the intended effect. Margot shrugged out of my hold and made an attempt to stand on her own. "I'm not *your* honey."

"Believe me, I know. If you were my honey I would have fucked the uptight out of you a long time ago."

As expected, she let out a shocked gasp, and put a few more feet between us. "I can't believe you just said that!"

"Really? You think I'm a useless bum, but the word *fuck* is a step too far?" I snorted and shook my head. There was no point rehashing just how little she thought of me. "Cash or card?"

"Right." She bent down and picked up her purse, which was empty, the lipstick, compact and money clip were all still on the bar floor. "Well, that's not going to work." She bent over again and her legs wobbled a second or two before they gave out completely.

"For fuck's sake woman," I growled and jumped over the bar to pick up the unsteady woman and set her in a booth so she wouldn't hurt herself or my bar furniture. "Stay."

"Don't order me around like a dog," she called after me, but I ignored her. "Hey, where are you going?"

I stopped at the door without turning to look at her. "I'll be right back."

"But *where* are you going?"

I pushed open the door that separated the bar from the kitchen and storage areas and stepped inside. Despite what princess high and mighty thought, grease was exactly what she needed to sober up enough to get her the hell out of my bar. Fifteen minutes later I returned with two plates piled high with food that paired perfectly with a night of drinking. "Eat up," I ordered brusquely and sat across from her to dig into my short rib nachos.

"I am not going to eat this!"

I nodded. "You damn well are, at least if you don't want a pounding headache, dry mouth and blotchy skin tomorrow. Hangovers are not fun after thirty."

I knew the argument would sway, her but still Margot was a stubborn woman and she took her time, mulling over her options. Looking and feeling terrible tomorrow, or sharing a greasy bar meal with me. "Fine, but I am not eating the bun," she announced and pointed at the burger.

"The bun is what will help soak up the alcohol." I filled another nacho high with toppings and chewed it, nodding at her burger and fries. "You know if you added some exercise to your day you wouldn't have to eat like a bird."

She glared at me as I continued to eat, ignoring her anger mostly because I was used to it. Eventually she picked up the burger and put it to her lips. "My god that is wonderful!" She let out several erotic moans and groans as she ate and I was thankful the table covered the effect her sounds had on me. "Mmm, so good." The words came out on a guttural growl that old me there was more beneath her prissy surface than she wanted the world to know.

I pushed the tall glass of water in her direction. "Drink."

That stopped her from inhaling her food just long enough to glare at me and give me a piece of her mind. "Is that how you talk to all women, monosyllabic orders just barked at them?"

"Only the hard-headed ones who don't listen. Water will help so you don't feel like ass tomorrow."

"*Must* you be so vulgar?"

"I don't have to, but you get so bent out of shape about it that it's just fun. And I don't make fun of you for talking like you're some etiquette teacher at an all-girls school in the Fifties. Do I?"

"It's called manners," she said primly, and wiped ketchup from the corner of her mouth as she eyed my nachos. "Do you mind if...can I taste your nachos?"

The fact that she even asked surprised me, but I nodded, and took my time finding the perfect chip to pile high with barbecue short ribs, sour cream, cheese and of course, jalapenos.

"Go on. Taste."

Her breath hitched, and her violet eyes darkened with desire—for me or the food, I couldn't tell—and she opened her mouth to accept my offering. I slid the chip in and her lush lips closed around it, her tongue swiped part of my thumb before I released the chip and sent a bolt of electricity straight through me. I watched as Margot closed her eyes and chewed, savored all the flavors of one of my best selling dishes.

"Good, right?"

She nodded, and one silver tendril fell loose and curled around her collarbone as she swallowed. "Wow, that is delicious! Really delicious."

It was on the tip of my tongue to say something sarcastic, but I resisted and turned my attention back to the nachos, piling another chip to make sure I had a little of everything on top. Margot grabbed my wrist and I looked up with a frown.

"What's wrong?"

She tugged my wrist with a smile and brought the chip to her mouth. She nodded more vigorously with every bite, and as she finished, a smile spread across her face. "Oh my! It's even better on the next bite. Absolutely wonderful!" Her eyes lit up beautifully, and I glanced away for a brief moment and then looked back, just to reassure myself it was the same woman, because this woman, a little bit tipsy and full of smiles for me, was not the Margot I knew. I wasn't sure if this was the alcohol, or a facet of her personality she kept hidden in favor of the stuck up persona she showed the world. She noticed me staring and her eyes widened in shock. "What? Oh, sorry that was terribly rude. It's tasty though."

It didn't seem to pain her at all to offer up a compliment about my bar, so I smiled and switched our plates, taking the loaded burger and curly fries for myself. "Enjoy."

"Oh no, I couldn't possibly let you give up your dinner for me."

I waved off her concern and popped a fry into my mouth. "Consider it my birthday gift to you."

Her shoulders fell in resignation and Margot nodded. "Thank you, Grady. That's really sweet."

I shrugged off her words, knowing the alcohol put her manners before her dislike of my lower status. "No problem. Eat."

We ate in silence, until the plates were clean, and I cleared them to the kitchen, returning with more water for Margot and the birthday cake Nina dropped off earlier. "What's this?"

"Cake. Nina made it for my birthday, and since it's also your birthday, you can have a slice," I told her and hesitated. "Unless you don't eat sugar either?"

"Funny," she rolled her eyes. "I indulge in sugar occasionally, especially on my birthday. And today of all days," she groaned and attacked the slice of two-tiered cake with her fork.

"Happy birthday to us," I said and attacked my slice with the same energy. Nina's cake was delicious with a layer of vanilla and a layer lemon soaked in hazelnut liqueur. The buttercream frosting made my mouth water even as I ate it.

I noticed that Margot had stopped, and I knew instantly something was wrong, but I kept my focus where it belonged, on my cake. At least that was the plan, but then she burst out in tears. Not the soft, quiet tears I'd have expected from her, but big, wrenching sobs that shook her petite frame until the plate in front of her rattled.

"I'm sorry," she bawled. "Don't mind me."

As if it were really so simple to just ignore a beautiful, bawling woman while she cried her eyes out. With a quiet groan, I pushed away from my seat and rounded the booth to sit beside Margot and wrap my arms around her.

"It's all right," I whispered, and ignored the press of her plump breast against my chest as I rubbed soothing circles against her back while she cried and cried. Eventually she needed oxygen, or maybe the tears were coming to an end, but when I pulled back, she looked up at me as tears still swam in her eyes. "Tell me you're not one of those women crying because you're getting older." I smiled in relief in the face of her wicked glare.

Margot was back.

CHAPTER 3
MARGOT

I don't know if it was part of his plan or not, but Grady's words stopped my tears instantly. I glared up at him, all too aware of just how close we were. So close that I could see the threads of light blue and dark blue that swam together to give his eyes their unique hue. I blinked hard to swipe my mind free of his handsome face, and gave his chest a shove, which did nothing, because the man was a big as a house.

"What in the hell is that supposed to mean?"

His lips twitched with laughter. "It just means that I hope you're not sad about living another year. Aging is something none of us can avoid, no matter how *hoity toity* we are."

I snorted at his glib words about aging. He wasn't just a man, he was a young and good looking man. "This coming from a man who's barely thirty, if he's a day."

"Thirty-two as of today, thank you very much." He flashed a wide grin that was equal parts handsome and annoying.

I rolled my eyes at the pride in his eyes, the easy way he just blurted out his age. "Come to me when you're pushing fifty. Not that *I'm* fifty," I rushed to clarify. "I'm forty-seven and even that number I share reluctantly."

"And?" There wasn't a hint of surprise in his voice, or revulsion either. "You sure as hell don't look forty-seven, and who cares if you do. You're successful, beautiful and rich, that's enough for any man. More than enough."

His words stunned me, mostly on account of our contentious relationship, which was admittedly, mostly my own doing. "That's really what you think? I don't need compliments because you caught me crying."

Grady laughed. "Believe me, I wouldn't lie to make you feel better." He flashed a slow and sexy smile that sent heat flaming throughout my body. "Stuck up as hell on top of everything else," he added with a wink. "It's all true."

That's why I believed him, because for all of his faults, Grady was an honest guy, especially where I was concerned. He never hesitated to tell me what he thought of me, good or bad. Mostly bad, given our relationship, and for that reason his compliment touched me even deeper.

"Thank you Grady. Really." Before I could think better of it, I wrapped my arms around his neck and squeezed him tight, all too aware of the mounds of rock hard muscle. My nipples tightened with arousal, and when he hugged me back, that earlier heat turned to an inferno charged with pure electricity. I pulled back with a gasp. "Thank you."

He didn't linger on the hug thankfully, and slid from my side of the booth and returned to his side. "You can't cry over cake."

"I thought it was spilled milk," I told him, and sat up a little taller when an amused grin split his face, teeth so white and stark against his tan skin and red beard.

"I say never cry when there's food in front of you. It just feels wrong." He shrugged again and finished off his cake in four enormous bites before he turned his gaze to me again. "So why were you crying if it's not about aging gracefully?"

I shoved a bite of cake in my mouth and chewed slowly. It was sweet and rich and fluffy, and the perfect distraction. But Grady was an expert at waiting people out, and after another bite of cake, I found myself telling him everything. "My last ex-husband Michael left me for our mechanic, Adam. They fell in love and have been living their happily ever after since the divorce, before the divorce if we're being honest." And apparently I was being totally honest with my sworn enemy. "And today he decided to share his *wonderful news* with me, that he and Adam have adopted adorable twin girls." Saying it out loud left a nasty taste in my mouth and I gulped some water.

"Are you still in love with him?"

I laughed. "Goodness, no. The divorce was necessary and inevitable, only I didn't see it until it was too late. Michael did the right thing by initiating the divorce, because he knew I never would."

Grady's brows dipped in confusion. "But you're not in love with him?"

"No," I laughed. "I love Michael, and I probably always will. We were, and mostly are, still great friends, but we should not have mistaken that for the kind of love that leads to marriage. It was just my own dumb luck that by the time I figured it out, my years of having children were behind me." And that was the part I couldn't get past, wouldn't forgive Michael for taking from me.

"Says who?"

"Says who, *what*?"

"That your years of having kids are behind you? It's not the eighties anymore Margot, women are having kids well into their fifties, especially women like you. With money."

I shook my head at his words, all of them. "You can't be serious. A woman my age, pregnant?" I laughed.

"My mama's friend Charlene is fifty-six and she has a one year old boy. She and her second husband have been together for a few years and weren't trying, but one day she just popped up pregnant."

I couldn't deny how much his words filled me with hope, but hope was a bad thing for a woman like me, a woman my age with no prospects for a man. No desire either. "Definitely fertility treatments," I said dismissively.

"Doubtful, since Mama called him an oops baby." He shrugged. "She's like an aunt to me, so I didn't get into specifics about *how* she made her baby. The old-fashioned way I assumed." Grady distracted me for a moment by taking the last bite of my cake. "Anyway, all I'm saying is that it's not too late if you really want to have kids."

I sat there and stared at him, shocked by his words and the kindness I hadn't earned. "Thank you for saying that. I don't deserve your kindness and I am well aware of that, but I think I needed to hear that."

Grady stared at me, and I wondered if he was counting my wrinkles because he was silent for so long. He took his time to clear the table and wipe it down before he handed me another bottle of water. "Drink." Before I could tell him to stop barking orders at me, he turned and bent over to pick up the contents of my purse, and I was struck speechless at the sight of his backside.

It was firm and round, and the tightness of his jeans hugged his thighs in a way that would make any woman get ideas. He wasn't just a big man, he was fit and graceful, like a lion had taken the form of a man. He turned and handed me the items in his hands. "Um, thank you."

He gave a short nod. "Let's get you home."

I shook my head and dropped my lipstick, compact and cash into my purse. "That's not necessary. I am perfectly capable of finding my own way home."

He sighed and clenched his jaw in irritation. "Yeah Margot, I know that you know how to get to your house. But it's late, and you're not exactly sober."

"Not sober, no, but the water, food and the sugar helped. I'm tipsy, if that. And I don't need a knight in shining armor."

He laughed, but it wasn't a real laugh. "Good, because I'm nobody's knight in armor, or in anything else. I'm just a concerned citizen helping out one of my own, because that's what we do here in Carson Creek, isn't it?"

I nodded, surprised by his spirit of community. He'd been in town for a few years now, but still most people—myself included—considered him an outsider.

"And if you don't come willingly, I'll be forced to throw you over my shoulder and strap you in. Either way is fine by me, sweetheart." He strolled away, a move that offered another excellent view of his firm backside encased in perfectly worn denim.

I was half tempted to test out his threat, but there was a reason that I kept my distance from him, that I made sure we never got too close or too friendly. Grady was too much man. He was too hot, and too masculine and too darn charming. He oozed enough sex appeal to fuel my late night fantasies, and after Michael I'd sworn off men. Permanently. "Fine," I told him agreeably when he returned, and stood with my purse clutched to my chest as if it were my virtue.

"Good girl," he growled and put a hand to my lower

back, giving me gentle nudge down the back hall of the bar and through the rear exit.

I stopped a few feet away from the gorgeous sparkling royal blue vintage sports car with the stark white racing stripes down the middle. "*This* is your car?"

Grady scowled at me and his hand fell away from my back, leaving me cold. "What's wrong with my car? Not fancy enough for you? Not luxurious enough?"

"Nothing," I sighed, realizing that he'd misunderstood my question, or not, I guess based on our history. "I guess I expected you to drive a giant pickup truck, or maybe an SUV."

He folded his arms and stared me down. "On account of me being such a redneck?"

"No, because you're such a giant of a man that I didn't think you could fit in something so small."

His lips twitched once and split into a smile which quickly turned into a laugh. "That's what she said."

I blinked at the joke, and a second later my own laughter bubbled up as I realized what I'd said. "Funny."

"Yeah," he sighed and opened the passenger door for me. "I'm very flexible," he said and wiggled his eyebrows. "And it's roomier than it looks."

I slid into the buttery white leather of the passenger seat and hummed appreciatively. "Nice," I told him sincerely and wiggled my butt against the plush seat. Grady closed the door and I took a moment to look around the pristine car, I realized he was right, it was downright spacious. "Did you fix this car up yourself?"

"Some. My kid sister did most of the restoration. She's a mechanic and specializes in restoring classic and antique cars, in case you want to get revenge on your ex." He grinned and I smacked his thigh as his words sank in. "Too soon?"

"No. Is she beautiful?"

"She's my sister," he grunted. "And she's twenty-five." He squirmed in his seat and turned the key which produced a loud rumble underneath me.

"I could be a cougar. Carlotta told me so."

Grady's gaze went to me at the stop sign, his blue eyes raked in every inch of my body with appreciation and his hands gripped the steering wheel tight. "No doubt about that. Just, not with my sister."

I laughed. "Protective much?"

"Over protective," he corrected and maneuvered the car towards my small Georgian revival style home. I'd spent a great deal of effort renovating and decorating it to make it my own, knowing Carson Creek would be my forever home after my divorce from Michael. "This is you, right?"

I nodded. "Yes. Thank you for the ride Grady. And for the undeserved kindness."

He grunted in reply, and I made my escape before the man did something crazy like walk me to my door. Thankfully he didn't do that, but I was more than aware of the car idling in the circular driveway while I searched my clutch for my keys. "Lipstick. Cash. Compact. Breath mints. NO keys." I went through the purse three more times just to make sure before I returned to Grady's car. "I don't have my keys. I'm sorry."

He sighed and leaned over to push the passenger door open again. "I guess that means you're bunking with me for the night."

"What? No! That isn't necessary. I'm sure they're on the floor of your bar somewhere."

"I'm exhausted and my house is that way," he pointed in the opposite direction of the bar and patted the seat. "My place or nothing Margot."

I knew he meant what he said, and I didn't want to repay his kindness by being difficult, so I dropped into the passenger seat and nodded. "Thank you. I feel like I'm saying that to you a lot tonight."

"Hurts, doesn't it?"

Not as much as I thought it would.

CHAPTER 4
GRADY

Margot was inside my home, which was not something I ever thought would happen, but now that she was here and looking around, I braced myself for whatever criticisms she might have. Not that I cared. I found the American farmhouse within days of buying the bar and fell in love with it. After a year of updating the plumbing, heating and light fixtures, it was home. I loved it, and with Carlotta's help it was nicely decorated in what she called masculine colors. It looked like an adult male lived here, not a bachelor or a college kid.

I set the alarm out of habit, even though it was mostly unnecessary in Carson Creek, and kicked off my boots determined to brush off whatever cutting remark was about to fall from Margot's lips.

"This place is nice," she said on a sigh and looked up at the exposed wooden beams. "Very masculine."

So far, so good. "But?"

She turned to me with a knowing smile. "Could use more personal touches. This could be a model home for the lack of personal details, but it's nice."

"I'll let my decorator know," I grunted in response, because I was expecting snooty and critical, not complimentary. I smiled at her shocked expression. "Tired?"

"Thirsty."

I nodded for her to follow me into the kitchen. "Flat or sparkling water?"

"Something stronger."

I turned from the fridge and watched her as she watched me, a small smile on her lips. "Beer." I pulled two brown ales from the fridge and set one in front of her frowning face. "It's beer, or it's water."

She eyed the bottle as if it might jump up and bite her, and I reached out to put it back in the fridge. "Wait." Her hand shot out and grabbed my wrist the same as she had at the bar. "I'm not being critical, but beer has too many calories."

"A few extra calories won't kill you Margot. Just walk a few extra steps tomorrow," I growled and popped the cap on both bottles.

She eyed the bottle carefully and read every word on both sides of the label, still trying to find a way out of drinking it.

"Margot?" She gasped as if startled and looked up at me. "Michael and Adam's twins are probably really adorable. Probably even have those matching bonnet things with their names on 'em to tell them apart."

She growled and picked up the bottle, taking two impressive gulps before she slammed it down on the kitchen table with sigh. "That wasn't very nice."

"But it did the trick," I told her and set my beer down and headed back to the living room to grab a bottle of whiskey from the bar. I poured two shots and handed one to her. "Didn't it?"

"Jerk," she growled and accepted the shot, which she knocked back impressively. "Yeah, that hit the spot."

I set the bottle down between us and dropped down into a chair with a grunt. "So Margot, if you want kids, why have you waited so long?"

"You mean my age?"

I shrugged. "No, I mean you've been divorced for a while now, so what's with the wait?"

She contemplated her answer for a long time, and took a long swig of beer. "Honestly? I just didn't think about doing it on my own, and since I've sworn off men I figured that part of my dreams would simply go unfulfilled."

"You don't want a man?"

"Not really," she sighed and then sat up a little taller. "No, I don't. Michael and I were friends for a long time, and he wasn't honest with me about who he was. Unlike my other exes, I cherished his friendship, and clearly I misread everything, which is a mistake I refuse to make again."

"So because Michael struggled to admit his truth to himself, all men are liars?"

"Not all men, but I've been married and divorced three times. Clearly I'm not cut out for it."

"Hmph." This attitude was so at odds with the woman who carried herself with the grace of a royal that I didn't know what to say.

"Don't judge me Grady."

"You mean the way you've judged all men as unworthy because of three bad ones? Okay, I won't."

"Smart ass." She looked around the kitchen and finished off her beer in silence, but I knew she had questions.

"Go on, ask."

She frowned. "Ask what?"

"Whatever it is you're itching to know," I told her. "Your eyes give away everything your mouth doesn't say."

"They don't," she insisted, but I only stared in reply. "Okay fine. I'm curious how you got this house and the bar at your age?"

"I conned them both off an elderly woman."

She stared at me for a long time before she smiled. "Okay I deserve that, but to be fair I never said or implied I thought you were a criminal."

She hadn't. "You just think I'm beneath you."

"I don't actually, and that's all I'm going to say about

it." The pink climbing up her chest and neck to her face told me some of the story, and I didn't want to push for the rest.

"I won the lottery. Not the big Powerball, but enough to buy my mama a house. The bar, plus this house for myself, and I'll live comfortably for the rest of my life."

Margot studied me, probably trying to figure out if I was lying or not, and when she finally decided it was the truth, she smiled. "Wow. I've never met a lottery winner before."

"No autographs," I deadpanned and she laughed again. The sound was so fucking feminine I had to grip my bottle with more force than was required.

Margot yawned and I leapt on any excuse to get some space from this woman. "Excuse me."

I stood. "Come on, let me show you to your room."

"Lead the way."

I nodded and exited the kitchen, doubling back to the living room and up the staircase that would take us to the bedrooms. There were four bedrooms, two of them with their own bathrooms and I put her in the second one that was on the opposite end of the hall from my room.

"This is it. There's a bathroom attached, and it's got everything you need."

"Except something to sleep in," she said playfully.

I blinked and stared at her in the navy blue dress that hugged her curves. "You don't sleep naked?"

"No," she gasped and her cheeks turned red all over again.

"Too bad," I told her and rushed away from her until I was inside my own room, I grabbed a t-shirt and returned to the doorway of the guest room. "I don't have anything else."

She took the shirt and smiled. "This will do nicely," she told me.

"Good. I'll see you in the morning."

"Grady?"

I stopped and turned. "Yeah?"

"Thank you. Again." She closed the gap between us and placed her hands on my shoulders for leverage so she could press her lips to my cheek in a chaste kiss.

I noticed the kiss less than her soft curves pressed against me, her tits on my chest and my hands on her round hips. She had more curves than she showed, and my body liked them all. Enough to stand up and take masculine notice.

"No problem," I whispered in her ear, my notice and appreciation of her curves becoming hard to hide.

Margot gasped and pulled back, heat turning her violet eyes nearly black. "Grady," she sighed, but before I could offer up an apology or a non-apology, her lips were mine, her tongue sliding along the seam of my lips until I opened for her.

Too shocked to do anything but give my body what I wanted, I gripped her tighter and let her lead the kiss.

Her tongue slipped between my lips and danced with mine while her hands roamed all over my chest and back.

She moaned when my tongue joined the dance and pulled back to grab the hem of my t-shirt, which she yanked over my head and stared at my chest. "Beautiful," she sighed and ran her hands along my bare chest like it was a work of art and not a product of hard work. Her hands moved wildly and she attacked my mouth again as if she couldn't get enough, like she just couldn't help herself.

It was hot, the kiss, the woman and the encounter. I gripped her round ass in my hands and pulled her up against me to fit her against my cock. She gasped and wrapped her legs around my waist.

"Margot," I whispered in her ear. "Are you sure?"

She nodded and let her feet drop to the floor. "I'm sure," she said and gave me her back. I yanked the gold zipper until it stopped and shoved the dress over her hips and down her legs. I turned her around and my breath caught in my throat. Her lingerie, a dark blue lace one-piece, showed off cleavage and a small patch of hair, not to mention long smooth legs.

"Ah, fuck Margot. You're gorgeous." I picked her up and tossed her on the guest bed, smiling down at her when she squeaked surprise. "Come here." I tugged her legs until she practically hung off the edge of the bed, and spread them open.

She tried to close her legs, but I wouldn't let her. "You don't have to Grady."

I knelt on the floor and tossed her legs over my shoulders. "You don't want me to?"

"You don't have to," she said again.

"Okay." I bent forward and buried my face between her legs, licking and tasting her through the lace. The fabric rubbed against her plump lips and swollen clit with every swipe of my tongue, and her hips swirled against me, begging for more. Just like I knew she would, Margot tasted of vanilla and musk, like salted caramel, and I devoured her, enjoyed every gasp and cry and moan that left her lips.

"Grady," she panted and wrapped her thighs around my neck. "Oh my god!"

I smiled against her and slid one finger deep inside her pulsing channel and sucked her clit until she combusted completely. Her body shook and vibrated for long moments until her she went slack. I gave her one last lick and sat back to watch her.

"Good?"

"Great," she panted. "Excellent."

I smiled again and masculine pride surged through me. "Anything else?"

She nodded and pushed up onto her elbows. "Ready for more."

Exactly the words I wanted to hear, I stood and got rid of my jeans and boxers. The heat that flared in her eyes at the sight of me naked made my cock jerk and she gasped. "Like what you see?"

"Oh yeah," she gasped and nodded, mouth open before she licked her lips in erotic hunger. "Yeah. A lot. You're beautiful."

I smiled and knelt on the bed, which forced her to back up. I crawled on top of her and covered my body with hers. "You're the beautiful one," I told her and stole a kiss as my cock slid between her thighs, and rubbed against her slick opening before I pushed inside.

Margot gasped and I froze. "I'm good," she sighed. "It's been a while, and you're bigger than I...am used to."

I laughed. "Flattery will get you everywhere sweetheart." I pushed in slowly, inch by inch until my sac pressed against the smooth skin of her ass. "Good?"

She nodded quickly. "I'll be better if you start moving."

I gave Margot exactly what she asked for, exactly what we both needed. Hell, it was probably what we'd both been building up to for more than a year. She was tight and wet, two of my favorite qualities in a woman, and I was hungry for her.

My hips moved like they belonged to a man possessed, deep strokes, hard strokes that produced the wildest sounds from Margot, sounds that kept my cock hard as I pushed her to orgasm number two. "Grady," she moaned as it started to subside.

"Yeah?" I pulled nearly all the way out and slammed in hard as I gripped her hips so she couldn't move away, couldn't stop the pleasure that kept her nipples hard and her skin pink. "You want something else Margot?"

She shook her head and dug her heels into my ass cheeks. "This. Is. Good."

I smiled and changed the angle, lifting her legs to my shoulders and placing my thumb on her clit. She jerked up against me, hands grasped at whatever piece of skin she could touch as I thrust long and deep until I felt the telltale signs of her third orgasm creep up.

"Grady, please," she shouted.

My hips jerked uncontrollably as she came apart around me, pulsing hard enough that my sac tightened and my spine tingled as my own orgasm tried to claw it's way to the surface. "Fuck," I growled and tugged a nipple between my teeth.

"Oh! Oh!" Her body twitched and pulsed through the pleasure and I was so close the hairs all over my body stood on edge, and then moisture flooded between us and I was lost.

I jerked through my release and I clamped down hard on her nipple which earned me another shout of pleasure. "Ah, fuck," I grunted as the last of my pleasure spilled out of me.

Margot relaxed the moment I rolled to the side, and her breathing evened out within seconds. She was asleep, and I joined her moments later with a smile on my face.

She reached for me sometime in the night, or maybe it was early morning, first with her mouth on my cock, and then with her tits in my face as she rode me to her fourth orgasm. It felt like some kind of fever dream, the kind where you couldn't tell reality from fantasy.

But when I woke up the next morning to the note on the nightstand, *Thank you for everything. MBD,* I realized it had been reality.

A gloriously real fantasy.

Now it was back to real life.

And business as usual.

CHAPTER 5
MARGOT

One day after the most amazing, most earth-shattering night of my life, I had to slink back to Grady's Bar filled with embarrassment over how I'd thrown myself at him, how wanton I'd been in the throes of passion, to retrieve my keys.

I had headed to The Old Country House after leaving his bed since I always kept a spare change of clothes there. So I showered and prepared for the day ahead quickly. There was too much to do to let a small thing like humiliation stand in the way of checking items off my to-do list. The Old Country House had plenty of bookings, and the consultations usually started with me.

But finally, the last task on my list was unavoidable. So I took a deep breath and let it out slowly before I pulled on the door that led to the dim, blond pine wood bar. It was just after lunch, so the place was packed and filled with the delicious smells that I mostly ignored because they weren't part of my regular diet, but now the scent of barbecue sauce brought back more memories of last night. I had indulged in greasy bar food as well as the bar man himself.

But those nachos were the best thing I'd had in my mouth, aside from Grady.

I shook that thought off almost as soon as it occurred, straightened my shoulders and headed towards the bar determined to get us both back on normal footing. With my head held high I approached the bar and found Grady smiling and chatting with Carlotta.

"Is this your new de facto office Carlotta? You're here more than your office at The Old Country House."

She turned to me with smiling eyes and gave me a playful shove. "Margot you're such a kidder. All I need is my laptop and a flat surface, and this place has amazing sandwiches."

Sandwiches. How the woman was able to eat whatever she wanted and still maintained her magnificent curves was beyond me. "I'm sorry to interrupt, but I think I may have left my keys here last night."

Carlotta laughed. "Tied one on last night, did you?"

"You could say that," I answered with a smile. "I had a rough day yesterday and when I finally made it home, I couldn't find my keys."

Carlotta leaned closer and wiggled her eyebrows. "So

where did you stay last night? Or should I ask, with *whom*?"

I rolled my eyes at my nosy friend and turned back to Grady. "So, my keys? Have you seen them?" My tone was impatient and brusque, but it was only because of my shaky nerves.

Grady's blue eyes pierced a hole through me. He stared at me as if he could see my thoughts, before finally saying, "Nope." He turned back to Carlotta, a clear sign I had been dismissed. "So tell me more about these divorce parties. This is really a thing now, huh?"

"Yup." Carlotta nodded, her wide grin surrounding a bite of sandwich in her mouth. "They have become such a thing now that I need to come up with themes and décor to keep the customers happy, and there's not much on Pinterest to help a girl out. You ever been married?"

Grady scoffed. "Nope. Parents still married too."

"Well dammit Grady, how about you tell me what you would want if you were to have a divorce party?"

"Booze," he snorted with a shrug. "Maybe a hot woman to spend a night or two with. But I'm a guy, and I don't need streamers or themes to celebrate my freedom."

Carlotta laughed and opened her mouth to say something else, but my patience had grown thin. "My keys Grady, are you sure you haven't seen them?" When I had his attention, he fixed me with a bored stare. "You must have a cleaner, or a lost and found?"

He nodded towards the end of the bar. "Check the lost and found box, it's in my office."

"And your office is where?"

"Follow me," he barked.

I nodded even though his back was to me. He didn't look back once to see if I was following him, which was fine by me. I wasn't here for friendly conversation or to rehash last night's events, as incredible as they were.

"So where is this box?"

Grady kicked a box on the floor just inside his office. "If they're not in there you left them someplace else."

I nodded and squatted down as best I could in my A-line skirt to rifle through the box. I lifted up discarded scarves, a pair of sneakers and even a pair of jeans, but no keys. "You're kidding!"

"Listen Margot," he began and I turned and stood, eager to cut him off before he said something that might embarrass us both.

"Listen Grady," I said on top of his words. "Last night was great, amazing in fact, but it was a mistake. It shouldn't have happened and I think we should do ourselves a favor and forget last night ever happened."

His blue eyes stared at me angrily and his broad chest rose and fell in shallow breaths. "Already forgotten," he shot back and folded his arms. "Anything else?"

"Just my keys," I said and ignored the ache in my chest at his easy acceptance of my words. Maybe I hadn't made as much of an impression as I thought.

"I'm not your damned errand boy. If the keys aren't in the box, I don't know what to tell you. I gotta get back to work."

"It's not about you personally," I rushed to reassure him, and I was relieved that he didn't just keep walking. "I just think we're all wrong for each other. You're too young and I'm too set in my ways."

"Right," he snorted, shook his head and walked away, his long strides carried him away as quickly as they would without him actually running away from me.

I wanted to stop him and make him listen while I explained, but there was no point. It was best for both of us if we returned to our normal interactions, antagonistic and distant. So instead of going after him, I checked one last time for my keys before I gave up and left the bar without a word to Carlotta or Grady.

CHAPTER 6
GRADY

~J une
"I'll have a martini, and don't be so heavy handed with the brine this time." Margot was back to her old uptight self, barking orders at me as if I was her personal servant. She was damned lucky that I wasn't the type of guy to spread my business around town for public consumption, because I was so tempted to remind her that I knew exactly what she liked, and more importantly, *how* she liked it.

I smirked at her over the top efforts to pretend we hadn't been naked together a mere two weeks ago. "Sure thing ma'am. Only a slightly dirty martini, an untidy martini for you then," I sneered and got to work on her drink. I knew she loved how I made them, because she always ordered at least three, and uttered a little moan with her first sip. I took out my frustration on the cocktail shaker before pouring the liquid into a chilled glass and I slid it across the bar. "Enjoy your drink, ma'am."

She snatched the drink off the bar and made her way back to the table where Pippa, Valona and Carlotta had gathered for some type of girls' night.

"Wow, what was that about?" Levi's bewilderment was evident in his voice, and when I turned to him the shock on his face was almost comical.

"You know how it is with her."

"Yeah, normally you guys are a little snippy with each other, maybe even borderline rude, but that was outright hostile. What gives?"

"Nothing," I answered too quickly, especially considering the man had made a name for himself getting secrets out of people. "You know how Margot is, thinks she's better than everyone else, that we were all put here just to make her life easier." It's not like I was looking for happily ever after with her, or with anyone for that matter, but she didn't have to be so cruel about it.

"She's a little uptight," he agreed and sipped his IPA. "But you're both unflappable except when it comes to each other, and that has to mean something."

"Yeah it means we don't like each other, plain and simple. It happens, even in perfect small towns like this one."

"Nah," Levi laughed. "Lacey didn't like me when we met, and even we weren't like you and Margot. There's some serious sexual tension between you two, and a few nights together might be the only thing to fix it."

I shrugged and nodded as a pair of men flagged me down at the other end of the bar. "Nothing wrong that needs fixing," I assured my friend and tapped on the bar before I spent the next twenty minutes fulfilling orders and making drinks.

Occasionally my thoughts and my eyes would land on Margot, and I would get angry all over again. With myself and with her. I could almost hear my father's voice telling me not to be a pussy, and that horrible advice was the only thing keeping me from giving the woman a piece of my mind. That, and the fact that she wasn't worth it, and was well-regarded in town. It was best if I thought of her as just another notch on my bedpost.

That's all she was.

When I returned to Levi, his girlfriend Lacey had joined him. "What'll it be, Lace?"

She smiled and tapped her chin, doing that gears churning thing she did when she wanted to test my mixology skills. "I'm thinking I'll have a Rum Blazer, please." Her lips curled up into a mischievous smile and I laughed.

"Coming right up," I assured her and gathered the cocktail ingredients. "Planning to do a story in Cuba soon?"

"Nah, just keeping you on your toes. Whoa," she exclaimed as the blue flame appeared. "Wow, thanks."

"Anytime. Another beer for you Levi?"

"One of us has to find our way home later," he said with a laugh. "I'll just keep nursing the rest of this one.

"I'll be fine," she insisted and smacked a kiss on Levi's cheek before she turned a devilish smile my way. "So, you and Margot seem to be cattier than normal. What gives?"

"Catty? I have never in my life been accused of being catty. And nothing gives, just the usual around these parts." Everyone was starting to notice, which meant I needed to go back to ignoring her jabs. And her presence. And her curves.

"There's a first time for everything," Lacey said in a sing-song voice and pushed away from the bar. "I'm going to see what girl talk is going on." She left and my shoulders relaxed.

"The interrogation is over," I sighed.

"Better you than me," Levi agreed.

"Better you than Grady what?" Carlotta asked in that smooth as honey southern belle tone that fooled no one.

"Nothing," I replied, but Levi the traitor let the truth slip.

"Lacey was interrogating him about the increased tension between him and Margot."

"Oh that," she said and turned to me with a studious look. "A pitcher of margaritas please, two extra shots of tequila thanks."

"Got it."

Carlotta nodded and stared at me like she wanted to

say something else. I hoped she didn't find her words until I started the blender. "I think the problem is that you're just *so* much man. It's easier to hate you than it is to risk falling for your masculine energy."

I laughed and shook my head. "Masculine energy? You read too many women's magazines."

"Maybe so, but's part of the job. Anyway you ooze a certain type of virility, the most visceral kind, and Margot has been burned too many times to let a guy like you undo her."

"A lowly bartender?" Because no matter what she said, that was why she'd backtracked so quickly from a potential relationship I hadn't even requested.

"Nope, a sexy, tattooed bad boy who has BDE for days. And days." Carlotta stared at me with a teasing smile and I frowned.

"BDE?"

She leaned over the bar and motioned me closer. "Bick Dick Energy," she whispered in my ear before she pulled back with a threatening finger aimed my way. "If you tell Chase I said that, I will slice that energy up and put it in my trophy case."

"I promise not to tell Chase any of that."

"Damn right," she shot back and accepted the tray with a pitcher of margarita and fresh glasses on top.

"Tell me what?" The mayor stood right behind his girlfriend with an inquiring look.

Carlotta froze. "You are so dead Grady."

"Then who will make your favorite pastrami sandwiches?"

She shrugged and kissed Chase's cheek when he relieved her of the tray. "I'm sure there are other pastrami sandwich makers around."

"Not as good as mine."

"I'll make it work," she shot back.

I took a step back from the bar. "This conversation is over."

"Oh thank god," she sighed. "I actually came up here to talk to you about a couple of bookings, not your personal life or my sandwich obsession."

"Probably should have led with that," I told her with a teasing smile.

"Maybe, but giving you a hard time is just so much fun."

"Yeah, this is a blast," I deadpanned. "Tell me about the bookings."

"One's for the whole space, including the chairs out front and the terrace out back. It's Roman's local release party and the studio is tripling your usual rate."

"Triple?"

She nodded. "Yeah, it would be a good idea to get some more muscle around for that night."

"Got it. And hey, thanks for thinking of me for this stuff Carlotta." Business was good and I didn't need the extra bookings or exposure, but it was nice that she threw extra business my way just because she could.

"Of course. We're friends, you're good looking, which the clients appreciate and you make damn good drinks."

"Now you're gonna make me blush. Go on back to your coffee klatch or whatever."

She sucked in a shocked breath. "That is both sexist and old-timey, and I don't know whether to mock you or be impressed by your usage of old timey slang."

"How about you take your margaritas back to the table before they melt?"

She smiled cheerfully. "We'll pick this up later."

"We won't," I assured her as she and Chase walked away. I risked a quick glance at the booth occupied by the women, and now Chase, and stood a little taller, satisfied I hadn't even noticed Margot slip out.

It was progress.

Small, inconsequential progress, but in my book it still counted.

Right?

CHAPTER 7
MARGOT

"We have two more weddings lined up. One for end of August and the other," I paused as a loud yawn cracked my jaw. "Sorry. The other wedding is mid-September, and consultations have been set up for next week."

Carlotta looked at me brows knitted with concern and a curious expression on her face. "Are you all right Margot?"

I nodded quickly and slammed my eyes shut against the instant nausea that consumed me. "I'm fine, just a little run down. This summer is going to be great for all of us, Carlotta. It's everything I envisioned when I purchased this land." I leaned against my high-backed office chair and sighed. "I might have been pushing a little too hard to make it happen." The one upside to absolute exhaustion was that I slept like a baby every night. And I didn't have the mental energy to think of a certain blue-eyed bartender.

Carlotta sighed and leaned forward to put a hand on top of mine. "You don't have to do this alone Margot. We may own and run separate businesses, but we're partners and friends. If you need help, ask."

I nodded, grateful for her concern. "Thanks, but a little honest work never hurt anyone."

"Maybe not, but at our age we can't afford to be reckless with our health, physical or mental." With those words Carlotta un-crossed her legs and elegantly got up. She watched me carefully as she smoothed the flared out skirt of her purple dress and picked up her matching handbag. "The consults are in our shared calendar. Oh, and at the end of next month we have an engagement party booked, and they want to use the big house."

My eyes widened. "Really? Who?"

Carlotta's satisfied smile brightened. "Trey and Valona."

"Wow. Good for them." They seemed like a long shot at first, given the age difference, but they were by all accounts truly in love. And with their beautiful, blended family I wished nothing but the best for them. "That means we'll need to find a photographer for the event."

"Already on it," Carlotta said, half distracted by something just outside my office. "Take care of yourself Margot," she said and pointed a finger at me.

"I will. Promise." I had nothing scheduled for this

weekend, which was a blessing because it would give me time to catch up on things like sleep and laundry.

Less than a minute passed between Carlotta's departure and another knock on my door. I looked up full of annoyance that quickly shifted into surprise when I spotted the mayor at my door. "Is this a good time? Carlotta said you weren't feeling well."

"I'm a business owner, which means I'm always tired, but I always have time for the mayor. Have a seat and tell me how I can help."

Chase took a seat and flashed a friendly smile. "I want the town to sponsor a July Fourth barbeque, like a block party, but for the whole town and extra bonus points if we can get businesses in the area to donate something. It doesn't have to be enough burgers to feed the entire town, but here and there. You know?"

I nodded. "That's a wonderful idea. The businesses can get free publicity, while the town comes together to celebrate. And you can do a thank you speech before the fireworks."

Chase's eyes widened and he shook his head. "I don't think that's necessary."

"It is. Not only will the town want to hear from you, but the businesses will appreciate a special thanks from the mayor. It can be short and sweet Chase, but it does have to be done." I jotted down a few notes with details necessary to throw a party of this size. "Where do you want this to take place?"

"All over town. If people want to keep it simple and invite friends to their backyard, that's fine. If they want to do it in the park, or here or wherever else they think of, I just want them all to gather together to celebrate the holiday. And this will help some of the elderly and new residents to get out and meet new people." The smile on his face was filled with pride, as it should be, this was a good idea for everyone. "Can you help make this happen Margot?"

An event of this magnitude would require a lot of work with just two weeks of planning, but I would make it happen. "Of course. Anything else I should know?"

"Yes. I'm thinking of Movie in the Park around five-thirty or six with ice cream and dessert. A small break to set up for fireworks, and then we do them right in the park. Feasible?"

"I don't see why not, but I'll need to speak to your fireworks guy to make sure."

"You know him," Chase said with a smile. "For the past few years Grady has been the fireworks expert in town."

I shook my head in disbelief at my bad luck. "That can't be. He own's a bar, he's not an engineer or a pyrotechnician or whatever is required to do the job."

Chase shrugged. "According to Carlotta, that's exactly what he is. Speaking of, Carlotta is on board, but she said to check with you about use of the TOCH land."

I stared at Chase for a long time, hoping that he hadn't

just told me that Grady was the man I needed to speak with about fireworks. After weeks of keeping our distance, this couldn't be happening. Not now.

"Nothing's on the books for the holiday, and I'm happy to let the town use the land to celebrate our nation's independence. But I think for the sake of liability, that we get an actual pyrotechnician." With barely two weeks to get everything taken care of, this would be the perfect distraction from being tired and ignoring Grady. The stubborn man still made nightly appearances in my dreams even though weeks had passed since our night together, and since then he's ignored me when I was at the bar.

Can you blame him? That was the question I always asked myself when I wanted to get mad or sad about the entire situation.

"Margot?"

I blinked and flashed a half-smile at Chase. "Sorry. I guess my mind wandered a little bit. There's nothing to worry about, we're going to throw the best town-wide barbecue block party Carson Creek has ever experienced. I promise."

"You always make sure everything comes off beautifully Margot, but seriously, you're looking a little green. Let me get you a water or an energy bar. Something," he mumbled with barely concealed panic.

I stood and waved off his worry even though I did *feel* a little green. "Not necessary, I told you I'm fine. It's probably fatigue mixed with skipping over breakfast. And lunch." I tried for a smile to assuage Chase's concern, but my smile seemed to have the opposite effect.

"I'll get you some water," he said and darted to the small black fridge I kept in the corner of my office. He grabbed a bottle and walked back towards me with purposeful strides.

"It's fine Chase. You worry too...whoa." My legs wobbled and I started to sway a little, black dots appeared all around Chase's head just as my stomach lurched. I clutched my midsection and sighed. "I'm just going to finish my notes and call it a day," I said and swayed once before my legs gave out and everything went totally black.

CHAPTER 8
GRADY

"And what about your number handsome, can I have that too?"

A busty brunette with big green eyes leaned over the bar with perfectly painted pouty red lips, tits on full display as she batted her eyelashes at me. She was hot as hell, but I wasn't interested.

"What are you gonna do with my number? Give it to the man who gave you the ring hiding in those jeans?" Yeah the white strip on her left finger was a dead giveaway.

She laughed, mischief in her eyes. "What do you care?"

"I don't," I assured her in my flattest voice. "But I also don't sleep with married women. Sorry, not sorry."

A slow smile spread across her face as she shrugged and pushed away from the bar. "Too bad. But you know that noble streak only makes you even hotter." She smacked a twenty dollar bill down on the bar and sauntered back to the group of women celebrating yet another divorce.

I shook my head at the group of shameless women who flirted like it was a sport. They were all very good at it, and eager to practice at any given time. It left me exhausted, but entertained throughout the long evening of slinging cocktails for fifty partygoers.

"Last call!" The event ended at one o'clock, and with twenty minutes to go everyone would want one last drink or two before heading home, alone or with a temporary bed mate.

Any other night and I might have taken one of the single women up on what they clearly offered freely and solely for fun, but after a full day of working behind the bar and then late into the night for this party, all I wanted to do was to go home, take a hot shower and devour the stew in my slow cooker with fresh bread I'd gotten from the bakery.

"Hey Red, you have a girlfriend?"

I smiled and shook my head at the guest of honor. "I don't."

"Are you looking for one?"

I shrugged. "Can't say that I am, honestly."

"Good. Me neither." She slid her business card across the bar. "You look like a lot of fun for a few nights, and I am in need of that kind of fun. Call me."

I took the card and shoved it in my back pocket. "I own

the place so I don't have a lot of free time, but I always make time for fun."

"Excellent. Another round of shots for me and the girls. Whiskey and then blow job shots."

I smiled. "Coming right up. You have a designated driver?"

She sighed and leaned more against the bar. "You really are one of the good ones," she murmured. "We do and his name is Ricky. He drives the bus I hired for tonight."

"In that case, drink up and congratulations on your freedom."

"Thanks." The woman left an impressive tip and took the tray of shots like a pro in one hand and carried it back to her friends. "Two more rounds before we hang up our stilettos ladies!"

By the time one-thirty rolled around I was the last one standing inside my bar, thankfully. I swept the floors and wiped down all the tables, leaving the rest for the cleaning crew to take care of before lunch tomorrow. The kitchen was clean enough to eat off the floor and the bathrooms, well the cleaning crew would have their work cut out for them, because I sure as shit wasn't touching them.

I made sure the front door of the bar was locked and made my way towards the back exit where there were a couple spots reserved for employees, all of whom I'd sent home hours ago. The truth was the bar did enough business that I could hire more people, but that would cut into the hours for the men and women who relied on this place for full-time employment. College kids and single mothers in town were happy to fill in when they were needed, and everyone was happy, which made my life easy, and that made *me* happy.

"Grady!"

I turned on full alert and reached out for the person coming up behind me. It was Carlotta and I released her immediately. "Sorry. Don't sneak up on people in dark alleys."

"Sorry," she said, her eyes wild and her voice frantic. "How did the party go tonight? Sorry I didn't make it, but I was at the hospital and by the time it occurred to me to call, it was already so late, and I rushed right over," she said and sucked in a breath, presumably to jump back into her endless word vomit.

"Carlotta breathe." I put my hands on her shoulders and breathed in deeply and out slowly. "That's good. Are you all right?"

"Me? Yeah, I'm fine."

I clenched my jaw. "Then why were you at the hospital?"

"Oh," she rolled her eyes. "Right. Margot passed out in her office today. Chase was there when it happened, so he called me because Margot's father died a few years ago and her mother lives in one of those retirement villages in Florida and Margot didn't want her to worry."

"What's wrong with her?"

"Don't know," she said and looked away. "I saw the light on so I stopped, but I'm headed to Margot's place for a change of clothes since they want to keep her overnight."

"Overnight? That's not *nothing*, Carlotta." For a brief moment my heart squeezed at the idea of something being truly wrong with Margot. She was a snob, but she wasn't a bad person, I'd seen her go out of her way to help nearly everyone in town who needed it. It was just that her and I were like oil and water, we simply did not mix.

Carlotta waved off my concern. "She hit her head when she passed out so it's just a precaution." She looked away again, but not before I caught a flash of something that looked like guilt on her face, but I had no idea what she would be feeling guilty about, so I shrugged off the thought. "Anyway, did tonight go well?"

"It went perfect. The partygoers drank a lot, and some even ordered food without bitching that it wasn't included in the event. They paid happily and tipped generously, filled their bellies and offered their compliments to the chef."

"Great. Good. Excellent," she nodded. "I should have called. I'm sorry."

I brushed off her apologies. "Nothing I couldn't handle Car. It's late, you should get going if you want to get back to Margot." For a brief moment I thought of offering to drive her back to the hospital, but I was literally the last man on earth Margot would want to see when she was in such a vulnerable state.

"Thanks Grady. You're the best." She jumped up and kissed my cheek and took off towards her giant SUV.

I couldn't help but smile as she tore down the narrow alley in her oversized vehicle, eager to get back to her friend. Carlotta was a character, much like most of the people in Carson Creek, which made me wonder if that's what people now said about me.

It was late by the time I finally sat down on the sofa to eat my stew and sort-of fresh bread while I binge watched a few episodes of a space drama. The stew wasn't as good or as hot as it had been in my fantasies, the bread was almost stale now, and the show didn't hold my attention for long, and it was all Margot's fault.

My thoughts wandered to the hospital, and I wondered if she was all right. Adults didn't just pass out for no good reason, it was usually a sign that something was very wrong.

Or she passed out because the stubborn woman is too damn concerned about her figure. It was a fine figure for sure, slender and curvy in all the right places, but it wasn't worth starving herself for.

"Not my problem," I grunted to shut off the endless stream of thoughts that revolved around Margo and made my way up to bed, where she appeared in my dreams, naked and sweaty and screaming my name, begging me for more.

CHAPTER 9
MARGOT

"I'm sorry, but you're going to have to repeat that, because I couldn't have possibly heard you correctly." I shook my head at the doctor standing at the foot of my bed with a sympathetic smile on his face.

"Margot," he began with an indulgent smile.

"No," I folded my arms in stubborn refusal. "I hit my head, and you're making me stay overnight, so you're going to have to say that again." My heart raced as the silence between us stretched, and I knew it wouldn't return to normal until the doctor confirmed he was joking.

"It's possibly a mild concussion Margot, not exactly an injury that produces memory or hearing loss." His lips twitched, and if my head didn't hurt so bad I might have lunged across the bed to put my hands around his neck. "But I'm happy to give you the news again. You, Margot, are pregnant. About eight weeks based on your hormone levels, but you should see an OB to be sure."

"That's not possible, Dr. Hines. I'm *forty-seven*." I whispered my age as if the doctor didn't have all of my information on the chart in his hand.

"I'm aware of how old you are Margot, but I am also aware of what the blood test indicates, and elevated hCG is a pretty good indicator of pregnancy."

"Pretty good?" I hopped on those two words like a drowning woman. "So not an absolute guarantee? It could be something else," I said, satisfied that more tests would likely be needed, because as much as I wanted a child, this was not how I pictured it, or how I wanted to bring a child into the world.

The doctor sighed, but he did a good job of concealing his frustration. "No. You're pregnant Margot. If this is an unwanted pregnancy we can talk about that, but don't fool yourself into thinking this is something else. It's not. Do you have any questions?"

"Only about a million of them," I nodded. "Is it safe to get pregnant at my age? Am I, or the baby at risk of…anything?"

He grinned. "There are certain risks associated with a geriatric pregnancy of course, but you're in good health with age being your own risk factor. An obstetrician can answer these questions better than I can, and I recommend you make an appointment right away."

"Geriatric? Did you seriously just say *geriatric* to me?" I knew I sounded hysterical, but I couldn't help myself, the words pregnant and geriatric felt wrong in the same sentence.

"It's just a term used in reference to a pregnant person over the age of thirty-five."

"Thirty-five! That is the most absurd thing I have ever heard! Thirty-five is like a baby, it's the age you *should* be having children, and you're telling me that even then it's already too late for something I'm doing many, many years after the age of thirty-five?"

"Margot, calm down."

"I am as calm as I can be considering the words that keep coming out of your mouth, Doctor."

The door opened at that moment, and Carlotta strolled in carrying my Louis Vuitton overnight bag. "What's all the noise? Is something wrong?" Her gaze bounced between me and Dr. Hines. "Is she okay, Dr. Hines?"

"No Carlotta, I am not fine," I answered angrily. "Not only am I pregnant, but apparently I'm having a senior pregnancy," I growled.

Dr. Hines cleared his throat. "I didn't say senior, I said geriatric."

Carlotta gasped and turned an angry glare at the doctor. "That is not better. Apologize, right now."

His brows dipped in confusion. "Apologize for giving her medically necessary advice?"

"Yes. You've just given her shocking news, and on top of that, you called her old as dirt."

"Now that is not what I said," he shot back and took a step towards the door before he turned to me. "You need to know the risks Margot. If you want to carry this pregnancy to term you must be realistic about what that means."

My shoulders slumped in defeat and I fell back against the bed. "I know, and I'm sorry, but this isn't what I was expecting to hear."

Carlotta snorted. "I mean you obviously have had sex recently, so it shouldn't be that unexpected. Protection is necessary, but pregnancy is always a possibility."

My eyes slammed shut and I groaned. Protection. It was the only thing missing from that night with Grady. Shit, Grady. "Tell me this isn't happening."

"I thought you wanted a baby?"

"Not like this, and not with...not like this," I repeated because there was no way on this earth that I would admit I had a one night stand with my sworn enemy, and worse, that we hadn't done anything to prevent this very thing from happening.

Carlotta dropped my overnight bag on the floor and dropped into the plastic chair near the window. "Wow. We have a lot to talk about, after Dr. Hines finishes with you."

Hines blinked and then nodded, eager to get through his spiel and get away from the crazy hormonal pregnant geriatric. "I'll have a nurse bring you the names of a few OB/GYN doctors in the area. In the meantime you need to make sure you're eating a healthy diet, get enough exercise and pay attention to your body."

"Pippa just had a baby, and she's not much younger than you Margot, maybe you should see her doctor?"

"Thanks. Maybe I will." Pippa had a baby recently, and she was fine during her pregnancy, if a little irritable, and had given birth to a beautiful baby girl.

"Congratulations," Dr. Hines offered hesitantly. "Call if you have any questions." Before I could utter another word, the man left my room so fast I wouldn't be surprised if he'd left skid marks on the floor.

"Yeah, thanks," I grunted to the door and turned to Carlotta.

Her face was lit with excitement and curiosity. "Tell me everything. Who is this mystery baby daddy?"

I shook my head. I couldn't tell her or anyone, not even Grady. Admittedly that was an impossible task in a town as small as Carson Creek, and if I didn't tell him, someone else likely would once word spread. How would he react to the news? Would he pack up and leave town, or would he step up and want to parent this child?

"Oh my God," I practically shouted before I gripped my aching head. "This isn't happening."

"Oh, it's that juicy? Tell me!" Carlotta smiled and stood to push her chair closer to the bed and laid a sympathetic hand on top of mine. "Margot this is good news. However it happened, you are going to be a mom."

I smiled at Carlotta since we had bonded over our childless states many times over the years. "Thank you, and I am happy, or I will be, right now I'm shocked and stressed out."

"Let's start with the easy questions, how far along are you?"

"Eight weeks," I answered a little too quickly. "Or thereabouts according to the doctor."

"Okay," she nodded. "Eight weeks. How many lovers have you had in that time?"

I glared at Carlotta.

She laughed. "It's an honest question. Last I heard you swore off men indefinitely, and here you are, with child." She fake-gasped and squeezed my hand. "It is a vibrator baby?"

I couldn't stop the laughter that exploded out of me at her silly question meant to make me feel better. "Funny. No, definitely not from a vibrator." Grady was so much better that I didn't know how I would be able to go back to my reliable collection and find any satisfaction.

"Even if you don't want to tell me, and you totally *should* tell me, news of your pregnancy won't stay secret for long. There are at least nine elderly residents of Carson Creek in the waiting area with nothing to do but slowly and eagerly text the latest gossip to their friends."

"No."

"Yep. They probably saw you come in, and I'm sure Chase has checked in with them so they know you're still here."

"Not helping Carlotta."

"Just tell me who it is and you'll feel better."

I shook my head. "I can't."

"It's embarrassing? Is it Roman? He's a little young, but he's mega hot. Nothing to be embarrassed about."

"It's not Roman," I grunted. "Do I look like a cradle robber?"

"It's not cradle robbing when it's a hot celebrity," she clarified.

"It's not Roman Gregory," I growled.

Carlotta tapped her fingertip to her chin, deep in thought. "There aren't too many single men in town that fall within the appropriate age range, so really it's just a matter of elimination," she said more to herself than to me. "That eliminates the under eighteen kids and Gigi," she laughed at the mention of Lacey's cranky, elderly father.

"You're on a roll tonight," I told her sarcastically.

"Given the chemistry between you two, my best guess is Grady, except that you two hate each other." Her musings ended abruptly and she slowly turned to me with a wide-eyed expression. "You and Grady?"

"Carlotta, please."

"Oh wow, this is even better than I thought! How was it? Did your toes curl? Did you scratch up his back? Do those tattoos go beyond his arms?" She squealed and tapped her feet on the floor excitedly. "Don't keep the details to yourself honey, it's not good for your complexion."

I laughed. "You are truly shameless, you know that don't you?"

"Absolutely," she agreed easily. "Are you secretly seeing each other, or was this a one and done type of thing?"

"More like a three or four and done, but yes, emphasis on the *done* part." I told her about our conversation in the bar the morning after, and how angry he'd been. "I doubt this news is going to be welcome."

"He might surprise you, but even if he doesn't, he does have a right to know Margot."

"I know, but I don't want to talk about it, or deal with any of that right now." I would tell him when I was ready to share the news and not a moment sooner.

"Okay." Carlotta held up both hands with her palms facing me. "No more talk about pregnancy, I pinky promise. Let's talk about the night the baby was conceived, because I'm sure that's a far more interesting conversation." She giggled gleefully, and as much as I wanted to tell her to back off, I couldn't.

"You can't tell anyone Carlotta. Not even Chase."

She motioned zipping and locking her lips. "Your secret is safe with me, at least until it's no longer a secret, at which time I reserve the right to tell Chase everything."

"Fine," I groaned. "It all started with a call from Michael."

"Your ex?"

I nodded. "Yep. Called to tell me that he and Adam adopted twin girls."

"He didn't!" Her outrage made me feel better.

"Right? He did, and that's not all," I sucked in a deep breath and prepared to tell her the part I hadn't told anyone, not even Grady. "He asked me to be their godmother. Can you believe that?"

"What a jerk! I know you say you guys are friends, but that is beyond cruel Margot."

I nodded. It had been my thought exactly. "It's like he thinks being a godmother is the perfect consolation prize for not having any kids of my own. Anyway, it was my birthday and I was upset, let my guard down and lost my keys."

"And lost your clothes along with them?"

"No. Grady was sweet and let me stay in his guest room. He said something nice and I basically threw myself at him, which was bad enough, but now *this*."

"Well he didn't push you away, so I'm guessing he was a willing participant. What's the problem?"

"He is who he is, and I am who I am. We don't mix well."

"Apparently nudity is the key ingredient to you two getting along. Sorry, but it's true," she said when I glared at her.

That wasn't a strong foundation for any relationship, not even a co-parenting one. It would be too contentious, and I didn't want to raise a child like that. "I'm not going to tell him," I said, the worlds edged with finality.

"That is a horrible idea Margot, but if you need anything I'm here." She stood and smoothed the fabric of the same purple dress she'd been wearing earlier. "Now you better think of something to tell Chase, because he's going out of his mind with worry out there and he'll be barging in here soon."

I nodded and motioned for her to go get him. I could deal with the mayor right now.

The bartender? He would have to wait.

CHAPTER 10
GRADY

~ July

"I can't believe she's pregnant," one of my older bar patrons said aloud enough for the lunch crowd to hear. "And at her age? I mean, really!"

I shook my head at the gossip, because it ran rampant in this small town, traded back and forth like currency. "Here's your salad and your burger, ladies. Enjoy your lunch."

"Thank you, handsome." The two older women smiled at me and I nodded at them and walked back behind the bar.

"Seriously, who gets pregnant at that age?" One younger woman at the bar asked another.

"It's gross," the other replied. "She should have grown children by now, not painting a nursery. Seriously it's disgusting." She even gave a shiver as if her point wasn't clear and rude enough.

I stood in front of them and waited until the conversation was over, or at least paused, before I interrupted. "Lunch or drinks, ladies?"

Both women gasped at having been caught gossiping, even though it wasn't frowned upon to gossip about your fellow citizens in Carson Creek. Two sets of reddened cheeks turned to me, blushing furiously as they looked at each other and then to me.

"Both, I think. Right Jess?"

Jess nodded. "Yeah, how about a Jack & Coke for me, and the fried chicken sandwich special?"

"Got it. And you?"

"Spiked lemonade and steak salad thanks. And hey, just so you know, we weren't being mean or anything, just talking about the news of the day. Ya know?"

I shrugged as if it didn't matter to me, but I felt angry on behalf of whomever this older pregnant woman was. "Gross isn't being mean? I'm learning more about this town every day," I told them. "I'll be back soon with your drinks."

"Jerk," one of them grumbled behind my back and I shook it off.

It didn't matter to me what a bunch of small town gossips thought about me, but I was sure the anonymous woman they spoke of would feel differently if she knew. I stabbed the women's lunch order into the digital ordering system that went straight back to the kitchen and then made their drinks.

"Food will be up soon," I grunted and set their drinks down.

As the lunch traffic died down so did the gossip, and by the time the after work crowd filtered in for happy hour specials and pitchers—beers for the men and margaritas for the women—all talk of the woman too old to have a baby according to the gossips, disappeared.

Until the next day when it started up all over again, and with more vigor, and from all manner of sources. The gossip was no longer relegated to the tables populated by women, even the men had opinions on when a woman should have a baby—as young as possible—and what she should know about her baby's father—everything.

"What do you think Grady? Forty is entirely too old for any woman to have a baby, isn't it?" Fred, one of my most loyal drinkers, asked with a confident smile.

"Pippa is over forty and she just had a baby. If a woman can still carry a baby to term then she's not too old to do so. What about those seventy year old men having babies with twenty year olds?"

Fred laughed. "If you're lucky enough to land a twenty year old at seventy, you give her what she wants."

"Forty is sexual prime time for women, so I'd say same goes," I told him and my mind immediately went to my own recent night with a woman in her sexual prime. That night, I absolutely would have given Margot anything she asked for. *Except a baby*, my mind added in rebellion. She would be the worse person in the world to share a child with. Those glimpses of kindness and humanity weren't enough to override her constant need to judge anyone and everything as beneath her unrealistic standards.

Fred laughed again and pushed his empty glass towards the edge of the bar. "Hell, I guess you're right. If I find a hot forty year old naked and panting after me, I'd give her what she wanted."

"I knew you were a smart man," I told him as I refilled his beer. "This one is on me."

It went on and on like that for the rest of the week until it felt as if the whole damn town knew about this mystery woman's pregnancy, and had an opinion on it. By the time Thursday afternoon rolled around, two things had happened. First my curiosity got the better of me and I found myself ear hustling all conversations in search of the woman's name, just so I could let her know that her personal business had sent every tongue in town wagging. The second thing was far more selfish. I was grateful that it wasn't my name leading the gossip headlines in town. Not that I had anything going on in my life worth gossiping about, but the gratitude hit the same either way.

"Grady, my favorite bartender!" Derek Gregory strolled into my bar looking every bit like the superstar he was, and smiled as he dropped down on a stool. "How goes the drink slinging business?"

"Busy," I answered bluntly. "And I'm the only bartender around these parts."

Derek, as good-natured as ever, laughed and shook his head. "True, but you make one hell of a Midnight Cowboy. In fact, I think I'll have one while I wait for my lunch order." He reached behind the bar for a menu and I barely even grunted at him, because I'd grown used to it since he and Bella got together. "I'll have a tuna melt for Bella with extra cheese. A chili cheese bacon burger for Everest, and even though I shouldn't, I'll have the Tennessee Titan sandwich for myself with all the fixings."

My brows rose in shock. "Did you all run out of food at the farm?"

"Nah, but Bella is gearing up for three days of farmer's markets, so this is one less meal she has to worry about."

"I guess those playboy days really are over. For now."

Derek shook his head. "Not just for now, forever man. As soon as I can make it happen, I'm gonna get her down the aisle."

"Good for you. You mind spreading the word around, so I don't have to hear another moment of shallow gossip?" I shook my head and put his order in the computer before I started on his drink. "If I have to hear it for another day I might start watering down the drinks."

Derek eyed his Midnight Cowboy warily. "But not my drinks, right?"

My lips twitched in amusement and I shrugged. "That depends. You gonna help?"

Derek laughed and shook his head. "I gave up on that thankless task years and years ago. Not much goes on in a town like this, which is good. Except for when you're the person who has an interesting life. Before we were famous, me and my brothers were often the topic of gossip. Too often. Try to fight it, and *you* become the next target. Not maliciously, but people start to wonder why your panties are in a twist about something they've been doing forever."

"Makes me grateful I grew up in a big city where no one gave a damn what I did."

"That's the trade-off. Everyone cared and stepped in before any of us kids could get into any real trouble, but then you just have to put up with them talking about it until something more interesting comes along."

"Thanks for the tip." I loved living in Carson Creek today, but I'm glad my adolescent shenanigans were mostly anonymous and no longer remembered.

"It is too bad about Margot though." Derek shook his head, and it surprised me that he seemed sincere, which only triggered another thought.

"What's wrong with Margot?" She hadn't been into the bar for a few days, but I figured my expert cold shoulder routine had left her too embarrassed to risk coming in for a while.

Derek blinked. "Grady, you own a bar. The *only* bar in town I might add, so how in the hell are you so behind on town gossip? I live on a farm on the outer edges of town and even I've heard about her pregnancy. How did you manage to stay ignorant?"

Each of Derek's words hit me like a ham-fisted blow to the chest. All week I've griped about listening to the gossip and sympathized with the poor middle-aged mom-to-be, and it turned out it was Margot the whole damn time.

"You all right Grady? You're looking a little green, man."

"Yeah, I'm good," I told him absently even though the words felt like sawdust on my tongue. Margot was pregnant, and everyone knew. Except me.

Was she ever going to tell me? How did she think she would be able to hide it from me?

And then another thought came to me. Had she used me that night to make her greatest wish come true?

Thankfully Derek's order arrived before he could witness the inevitable emotional spiral about to take place.

CHAPTER 11
MARGOT

I stayed away from Grady's Bar for a full week, because I felt guilty enough keeping this huge secret from him, and because I didn't want to see that disdainful look he'd perfected when he looked at me.

But a week was long enough to deprive myself of those heavenly nachos. I was pregnant and middle-aged dammit, and if short rib nachos are what would make me feel better about the gossip that flew around town, then I would have them, even if it meant staring down the intimidating owner of the establishment that sold them.

I stood behind my desk and stared out at the well maintained pond that provided a perfect spot for wedding photos, and sighed. "Time to hike up my big girl panties and go get what I want." And what I wanted was food, specifically those incredible nachos. Not Grady.

Absolutely not Grady.

Sure he'd snuck into my dreams over the past few nights, but that's only because he'd been the one to break my man-fast, and no other reason. The sex had been good, incredible really, and I had been replaying it in my mind ever since. But that didn't change anything as far as I was concerned. Good sex was just good sex, but now I was having a baby, and I had no clue if he wanted a baby now, or ever. That was a thought and a conversation for another time.

Now it was time for nachos.

I don't know how long I stood just outside Grady's Bar with my hand on the oversized brass handle, but eventually I gripped the handle and pulled it open, and I walked inside with my head held high. I wouldn't let myself shrink in the face of Grady's steely gaze. I refused to do anything but sit at the bar to ward off any unwanted conversation and have my lunch in peace.

I grabbed a menu from the end of the bar and smiled. Even though I gave Grady so much grief about his grubby bar, I never once put my hands on a sticky or greasy menu here. It was a bitchy response to my attraction to him, I knew that, but it was a necessary evil to keep my distance.

If only I had kept my distance that night in May.

A shadow crossed over me and I didn't need to look up to know it was Grady. He was here more than he wasn't. But when I looked up into his angry and disapproving blue eyes, I bit back a sigh.

"Margot."

"Grady," I said as stiffly as I could.

He folded his heavily muscled arms across his wide chest and glared down at me. "Got something you want to tell me Margot?"

I froze for a second, and wondered if the gossip had reached him, but Grady was the kind of man to face problems head-on, and he hadn't directly asked me, so I shook my head. "Nothing other than my order. Just those short rib nachos and a lemonade, thanks."

He continued to stare at me as if he was waiting for me to say something more. "Right."

My shoulders sagged. "I didn't come here to fight with you Grady. I just need to eat, and if that's going to be a problem, make it to go. Please."

His icy gaze stared down at me for a long time, and my heart raced against my chest loud enough that I swore the whole bar could hear it. Finally, Grady shook his head with that familiar look of disgust on his face.

"I guess this is all your world, and the rest of us are just bit players. Everything is only about what you want and screw the rest of us, right?" He shook his head one last time without giving me the chance to say anything, and walked away.

I didn't need to ask the question though, because it was clear that the gossip of my pregnancy had made its way to Grady. He knew. He *had* to. It made sense that he'd heard the rumors, especially considering drunk people gossiped louder than the rest of the town, and I knew that everywhere I went conversations stopped abruptly and all eyes turned to me.

Everyone was talking about me, and not because of my work bringing The Old Country House to life, for helping to keep the town's economy booming, bringing big city dollars to our small town way of life. Nope, it was all about Margot being too old to be pregnant, and how sad it was that she didn't know who fathered her child. It exhausted me to hell and back, but I knew the gossip would die down and move on to something—and someone—else soon enough.

My reproductive state was nobody's business but mine, and I would keep my mouth shut until, or unless I had reason to share with anyone, for any reason.

"Hey Margot!" Carlotta squeezed into the spot beside me and the empty stool with a wide smile. "Everything all set for the July Fourth town party?" Her eyes stared at me with concern, and I resisted the urge to bite back tears.

I nodded and assured her all the details had been handled. "Vendors have their delivery locations and everyone has maps to all the places they can go if they don't want to celebrate alone. I'll do one final check of everything tomorrow just to make sure, but yes, everything is all set."

"If you need anything you know where to find me," she offered with a friendly smile that made me feel guilty over the uncharitable thoughts I'd had about her over the years.

Carlotta was the only person in town who had offered me sympathy and friendship instead of judgment, making sure I didn't overdo it for the sake of doing it all on my own. "I know where to find you. The Mayor's office."

She giggled. "Nah, mostly it's my office, because his place is too busy. Too many people coming in and out for a proper afternoon delight."

I laughed at her words, feeling a little lighter after the tense exchange with Grady. "You're a bit loony aren't you?"

Carlotta's eyes widened in surprise. "You're just realizing that now?" Her gaze slid behind me and I had no doubt Grady stood there, staring a hole into the back of my head, probably wishing horrible things for me.

A few seconds later a tall glass of lemonade sat to the side of my heaping platter of nachos, and one angry bartender growled at me. "Anything else?"

"No thank you."

"I'm here to pick up my lunch order," Carlotta beamed a smile up at him. "Make it to go, please."

"Already did," Grady answered with a half-smile. "Be right back."

Carlotta leaned in when Grady disappeared behind the swinging door. "What crawled up his butt?"

"Probably just me," I admitted. "You know he and I are like oil and vinegar."

"The perfect vinaigrette?"

"Water and oil, I mean."

She laughed out loud and shook her head. "That, my friend, is what the eggheads calls a Freudian slip. Maybe you two are more like oil and vinegar," she said thoughtfully and her gaze slipped below the bar to my belly and she gasped. "Oh. My. God. Does he know?"

"Carlotta please," I whispered and she snapped her mouth shut so fast it would have been funny if the situation wasn't so dire.

"My lips are sealed," she promised. "Just tell me if he knows."

I nodded. "I think he does, but he hasn't said so explicitly." I whispered the words even softer and gripped her arm. "You promise you won't say anything to him or anyone else?"

She nodded. "Oh yeah, I promise. Not just because we're friends, but also because I can't wait to see how this all plays out."

I turned to her and smiled. "That doesn't sound very friend-like to me."

She laughed. "That's because you're not used to having honest friends like me," she answered playfully and ducked in close. "Why wouldn't he just ask you outright if the baby is his?"

"Because he doesn't care." The answer slipped out unintentionally, but it was the inescapable truth. "He's young and unattached, and probably wants to keep it that way, which means having *the conversation* is unnecessary."

"Whoa, that is a lot of assumptions you're making.

Maybe, and hear me out, maybe he doesn't want everyone knowing his business. Or worse, maybe he thinks you're ashamed of him."

"No." It wasn't him, but rather how it all happened. I didn't care what the gossip in town said, but it felt wrong at my age to get pregnant from a one night stand. "That's not it," I insisted and turned my full attention to the still steaming nachos in front of me.

"No offense Margot, but it's a possibility. Think of your reputation after all." Before Carlotta could say more or I could ask her to clarify, Grady returned with a big bag of food for Carlotta.

"Lunch for two. Extra dressing on the side."

"You're the best Grady. I'll stop by later to talk about bookings after the holiday weekend. Bye!" She breezed out of the bar in a quick ball of energy and left me all alone with the man who hated me.

And hated the idea that he was going to be a father.

CHAPTER 12
GRADY

"Hey Mr. Grady, whatcha bring to the barbecue?" Levi's grandson Mickey greeted me at the back gate with a snaggle-toothed grin and an inquisitive expression.

I lifted the brown paper bag and grinned. "This? This is for grownups only," I told the little guy, my voice thick with regret.

"Aw man, everybody is bringing stuff for the grownups. What about me?"

I pulled a can from the bag and offered it to him. "You want a beer, kid? I think your mom and grandpa might have an issue with it, but if you really want it then I won't stand in your way."

Mickey scrounged his face adorably and shook his head. "No thank you. Did you bring anything else?"

"Hmm, did I?" I scratched my chin, happy to spend

some time with someone who didn't indulge in gossip and backstabbing even if only for a few minutes. "I don't know. Let me see if there's anything else in this bag." I pretended to rifle in the bag, lifting up the twelve pack as I scratched the side of my head. "Oh wait, I think I found something."

He gasped. "What is it?"

I handed a smaller bag to the little guy and grinned when he snatched it from my hands. "Look and see."

He pulled out a can of root beer and a snack cake. "Thank you, Mr. Grady!" He hugged my legs and I wrapped a hand around him. "Thank you!"

"No problem kiddo." I held up a fist and he balled his little fist up and tapped it against mine.

"Grandpa and Lacey are out back. Mom's working today."

I nodded and made my way further into the backyard, happy I'd gotten up early to deliver my volunteered items to their designated locations so I could relax most of the day with my friends. I wouldn't have to put up with calls from Carlotta or Margot, which meant the day was mine thanks to Mayor Carson.

"Mr. Grady?"

I stopped and turned back. "Yeah kid?"

"Did you hear about the new dinosaur that was found?"

I shook my head. "No. Wanna tell me about it?"

"I wrote a story about it, wanna read it?"

"I sure do. I'll be sitting down back here." Mickey nodded and took off like a jet.

"Grady! Come on over and take a load off." Levi smiled at me from his spot behind the smoking and sizzling grill.

I raised the paper bag so Levi could see it over the grill. "Got a spot for more cold ones?"

"Besides my belly? Yeah, the blue cooler under the table."

I dumped the beers out and took a cold one for myself before I found a seat close enough to chat with Levi. "So, what's going on with you Levi?"

"Trying to find a way to propose with Lacey that isn't too cheesy, but it's memorable enough. Got any ideas?"

"Me?" I laughed and shook my head.

"I just need to find a way to let her know that she's special to me, but in a way that won't embarrass her."

"Levi, she already knows how much she means to you because you show her every single day in so many ways. Asking her to marry you is just a way to solidify your commitment to each other. Just say a few nice words about how beautiful and smart and funny she is, and tell her you can't wait to start your married life together. Add in some good food and maybe some dancing, and you're good."

Levi looked up with a burger perched on the edge of his spatula and smiled. "When did you become such a relationship expert?"

I shrugged off his backhanded compliment. "It's a

professional curse. You hear enough relationship problems and you start to see patterns. Besides, I see all and I know all."

"Yeah?" Levi looked around. "Do you see where the damn buns are, because I can't find them?"

I laughed and pointed to the table behind him. "You really are nervous about this proposal. Maybe I should watch the grill and you can go do it now."

"Nah, I still need to think on it." He laughed and watched Lacey as she walked across the yard with a bright smile on her face as she greeted everyone who'd shown up. "I'll think of something special."

"I have no doubt, my friend."

"You've heard about Margot?" He asked, and I nodded.

"I've heard." And the woman still hadn't come to me to let me in on the supposed secret. "Everyone is talking about it." And they still hadn't let up on the issue of her age or the identity of her baby's father. They were all taking bets, guessing and gossiping nonstop, and still she left me in the dark.

In the fucking dark about my own damn child. She had to know I'd already heard the news, yet still she said nothing. I knew Margot was a snob, but I didn't know until this week just how cruel she could be when motivated.

I spent most of the afternoon listening to, not gossip, but concerned conversation regarding Margot and her pregnancy. Lacey wondered if she would still be able to work such long days when her body started to change.

Pippa hoped she wasn't too stubborn to ask for help, and Valona planned to force her to hire an assistant before it was too late.

These women, I realized, were the closest things to friends Margot allowed herself to have. She kept herself apart from people. Not the town, she was quick to volunteer to help wherever she was needed, but she didn't strike me as the type of woman to just show up at someone's house to chat or vent about her problems. She handled it all herself, and she thought she could handle this baby on her own—without me—exactly the same.

The more I thought about it the angrier I became. I didn't mind an independent woman, even a stubborn one determined to do things the hard way rather than ask for help. Hell, I kind of respected that. What I didn't respect is the *reason* she kept it all a secret was because she was ashamed.

Ashamed she'd gotten knocked up by a bartender instead of stockbroker.

Ashamed she's having a baby with a man beneath her station in life.

She was just plain ashamed, and that was something I couldn't respect, and the moment the barbecue wrapped up as most townsfolk made their way to the park for the movie and fireworks, I went in search of Margot. I had a few choice words for her, and since she forced me to come to her, she would damn well listen to what I had to say.

I spotted her within minutes at the park. She was as

pretty as a picture in her yellow dress cinched in at the waist, prim and proper though it showed off her mouth-watering cleavage. She laughed with Carlotta and Chase as if everything in her world was right and perfect, meanwhile I was torn up inside because of her.

"Margot," I growled. "Got a minute?"

She looked up and I could tell by the look in her eyes and the straight set of her lips that she was about to run away so I grabbed her arm. "What are you doing?"

"Making sure you don't run away, then again you're not exactly in the position to be running from me now are you?"

She froze at my words, but her eyes widened in fear. "I don't know what you're talking about," she growled and leaned in closer. "And please lower your voice."

"Are you going to run the minute I let you go, or will you stand here like an adult and talk to me?"

Her nostrils flared with anger or frustration, I couldn't tell, and I didn't give a damn. "How can we talk like adults when you're gripping me like an animal?"

I laughed. "If I wanted to be an animal I'd toss you over my shoulder and march you out of here in front of the whole damn town. That would really send tongues wagging, which is exactly what you don't want, right?"

At my words her body sagged in resignation. "Fine, I won't run."

I nodded and released her. "You're pregnant," I said plainly. "Isn't there someone you forgot to tell?"

"Don't worry Grady, I'm not expecting you to do anything."

"Yeah, that's pretty fucking clear by your silence," I told her through clenched teeth.

"I didn't mean it like that," she began, but I was done listening to her bullshit.

"I don't need you to explain it to me Margot. You've made your disdain of me clear for months now, and you might think you're better than me or you're ashamed you got knocked up by a guy like me, but guess what? None of that matters anymore. That baby in your belly is mine, and I damn well will be taking care of him or her."

She gasped and the sound was equal parts outrage and erotic. "I never said you couldn't, I said you didn't have to."

"I don't give a damn what you said, because you don't run things, not anymore. Be ashamed all you want, keep it a secret, but don't expect me to do the same."

"It's not necessary," she whined.

I smiled even though I felt like throttling the damn woman. "You're not listening. Your words mean nothing to me, because you've shown your true colors. You can still think you're above me, but you're not, you are a reckless and cruel woman."

"Cruel? I am not," she insisted angrily.

"What would you call letting the whole damn town gossip without coming to me and telling me you were pregnant? Did you think you could hide it indefinitely, and

I'd be too stupid to put two and two together? That I wouldn't care? Or was it just that you got what you wanted from me and now you expect me to disappear?"

She gasped again in faux outrage. "None of that makes any sense," she whispered. "How could I have possibly planned for that night?"

"Don't know. Don't care. What's done is done, and I will be there every step of the way, and if you try to stop me in any way, I promise you won't like what I do next."

"Is that supposed to be some kind of threat?"

"Yeah, it is, because that's the only thing you understand isn't it?" I shook my head. "Your secret is out now Margot, learn to deal with it or not, it's not my problem. Just know that I won't abandon a child of mine. Not ever."

She notched her chin high in the air, eyes lit with defiance. "And you're so sure the child is yours?"

I smiled again. "I'm not the one image obsessed here Margot, which means I have no problem getting into a very public paternity claim. Can you say the same?" My lips curled into a bitter grin as I soaked up the fear in her eyes and the way it vibrated her frame, and then I walked away.

This wasn't how I planned to become a father, and definitely not with the woman I pictured, but this was how it happened, and I wouldn't let my kid down.

Not ever.

CHAPTER 13
MARGOT

I hated uncertainty.

Not knowing what came next was its own special brand of torture as far as I was concerned, and not knowing when—or if—Grady would show up again after our Fourth of July blowout was causing my body to react in a myriad of ways. My stomach twisted in constant knots, my heartburn was off the charts, and worse than all of that, my anxiety combined with nausea meant eating was pretty much impossible.

I mean, how I felt was Grady's fault. He wasn't the type of guy to growl a bunch of promises at a woman and then go back on them. No, he was the type who faced his problems head on, which meant that he was biding his time, lulling me into a false sense of security so he could strike when I expected him least. He was looking for the perfect time to strike, I just knew it.

And since there was nothing I could do about it other than drive myself crazy wondering when he would show up next, and what he would say, I busied myself with work. I had a few tours scheduled for The Old Country House with prospective clients who were interested in booking the property for a variety of events, so I pasted a smile on my face and greeted them like any good southern hostess would.

"Welcome to The Old Country House, I'm Margot Devereaux-Blanchard and this gorgeous property is all mine. Are you folks ready to take a look around today?"

I went through the spiel three times, first with two soon-to-be married couples, and then one couple in search of the perfect anniversary venue to renew their vows, with a wooden smile on my face. I showed off every inch of the property and recited its storied history before I pulled out my trusty, oversized calendar with a hopeful smile.

Three solid bookings later and I sat inside my office, exhausted and hungry while I waited for Valona to show up for her appointment. I was tempted to ask her to bring me lunch, but that felt like taking advantage of our friendship, so I abstained and waited patiently as I ignored my hunger pangs.

A knock sounded on the door and Val breezed in wearing a dark green dress that showed off her slender arms and hid pretty much everything else. "Margot, sorry I'm running late, but Trey needed some attention." She wiggled her eyebrows as she breezed into my office and dropped down in the empty chair with an exaggerated flair. "So, what's up Margot?"

I smiled at the new and improved Valona, as I liked to call her. Since getting together with Trey, she had become a whole new woman. Happy and smiling with her eyes on a fulfilling relationship and career. "I wanted to talk to you about new photos for The Old Country House website."

She looked shocked. "More photos?"

I nodded. "There's nothing wrong with the old photos," I rushed to assure her. "But so much work has been done since they were taken, so many upgrades, and I want the website to reflect that."

"Okay," she nodded. "Now that all the flowers in bloom everything will have that liveliness to make people want to be here for all of their special events."

I smiled. "Exactly. Besides we have new lighting fixtures in the mansion, and Dark Horse has made some improvements to the outside terrace, so I think it's time we show off a little."

Valona sat a little taller and smiled. "I like to show off a little, and I think that's exactly what we should do. Maybe we can get Levi or Lacey in here to do a little write up about the changes?"

"That's a wonderful idea!" Excitement coursed through my veins and I was happy that work provided the perfect distraction from everything else going on in my life at the moment. "If you can make it happen, then I won't stand in your way."

Valona squealed with excitement and jumped out of her chair. "This is so great, Margot! Thank you so much." She rounded the desk and wrapped her arms around me. "And congratulations on the baby. It's all so exciting!"

I pulled back surprised at her kind words. Not because Valona wasn't a kind woman, but most of the town held an opposing viewpoint. "You're not going to judge me for my age or lack of a stable relationship?"

She laughed. "Stable? I had two beautiful girls inside a marriage, and I learned too late that it wasn't as stable or as happy as I thought. Does that make me love Bella and Bridget any less? Hell no. Don't let the gossip hounds get you down Margot."

"I won't," I said with a deep sigh.

"You want this baby, don't you?"

"More than anything," I admitted to her as much as to myself.

"Then it is wonderful news, and I for one am happy as hell for you! I loved being pregnant, well," she laughed, "I loved it about eighty-seven percent of the time."

"That's a pretty exact figure Valona."

She laughed. "Sometimes the food cravings and the swelling became unbearable, but otherwise, I loved it because I'd always wanted to be pregnant and have children. I enjoyed every minute of it."

Valona's words had the immediate effect of relaxing

me and calming my nerves. In that one moment I felt nothing but good things about this pregnancy, no matter what Grady did next. "I am happy. Nervous about everything, but happy. Incredibly happy."

"Then that's perfect. Enjoy it," she instructed with a wide grin that slowly faded. "Not to pry, but is the father going to step up, or are you going at motherhood alone?"

My thoughts instantly went to Grady and I sighed. "It seems as if he plans to be involved, but we'll see I guess."

"Good for you. Even if you aren't together, it's nice to have a partner in all of this, someone to lean on when things get overwhelming, because they will. And to know you have someone who loves your little bundle as much as you do and will protect it? That's such a relief, but here's a little secret, it won't keep you from worrying nonstop."

I laughed. "Thanks Valona. You have both given me hope and instilled me with a deep sense of fear."

"Welcome to motherhood."

Truthfully, she made motherhood sound even more wonderful than I imagined. With Grady being involved, *if* that happened, I could enjoy being pregnant and being a mother while knowing that if something happened to me, my baby would be safe and loved.

"Uh-oh, I know that look. I've given you a lot to think about, so I'll get going. I'll check my schedule and get back to you about days to shoot the new photos."

I nodded. "I'll walk you out."

Val nodded and we fell in step together as we silently

made our way out of my office and towards the front bank of windows that allowed sunlight to filter in until it faded completely. "I love this space so much, so many places for photos."

I had an idea, and it stopped my movement completely. "If you want to take advantage of shooting on the property, I'm amenable to that under the condition you use some of the photos to highlight the place for the website. If we can get more photographer bookings at a premium, that's good business."

Val's violet eyes widened. "Really?"

I nodded. "Of course. Why not?"

She shrugged, but I knew what she was thinking without her voicing the words. "It's incredibly generous, and I am happy to take you up on your offer. I'll even use Trey if his handsome mug will help us all succeed."

"Exactly." I laughed and my feet started to move again. "I know I seem like a hard ass, but I really do want everyone to succeed."

"I know," Valona assured me. "You have a hard outer shell but you're a softie at heart. The people you let get to know you know that too, Margot. I promise." She stared at me for a long time, and I started to feel uncomfortable, and when she hugged me again that feeling intensified. "We'll talk soon. Call if you need anything…oh!" Valona's gaze was on me so she didn't see the giant wall of man and muscle until she bumped into him. "Sorry. Oh, Grady. What are you doing here?"

His blue gaze was fixed on me, his expression unreadable. "We need to talk." He stared through Valona and his gaze never wavered.

My gaze remained fixed on Grady, but I was aware of Valona's confused look as it bounced back and forth between us. "Oh," she said and took a step forward before she paused again. "Oh," she repeated as understanding dawned. "I'll just get out of your way and we'll talk... soon." Valona stepped around Grady and turned to face me. "Good luck," she mouthed behind his back.

"Grady." His name came out in a flat tone that belied my surprise and slight joy over seeing him, because it meant he hadn't just said those words because they were expected. He'd meant them. "Come on in."

Grady nodded and motioned for me to lead the way, and I walked on wooden legs towards my office where I quickly sat down just in case my legs decided to give out.

"Grady," I said again, this time with a bit more enthusiasm. "What brings you by."

His fiery brows dipped. "We need to talk," he growled. "And I brought you lunch."

I smiled at Grady. He was gruff and kind all in the same breath, and I didn't know how to take that, or realize the impact it would have on me. "Thanks but you didn't need to do that."

He set the bag on the lone spot of desk not covered by papers and took the seat across from me. He leaned back, looking relaxed as if he didn't have a care in the world, one eyebrow arched in question. "So you've eaten lunch already?"

"No."

"Breakfast?"

I shook my head. "I had a few bites of oatmeal, but it's difficult to eat most mornings."

"Then you're welcome." He nodded, urging me to open the bag.

"What is it?" I peeked inside, disappointed to find that it wasn't what I hoped for. "No nachos?"

He laughed. "No. It's a shredded chicken, brown rice and spinach burrito with the works. It's healthy and contains everything you and the baby need."

I blinked. "Need?"

"Yeah. For the baby to grow, and for you to have energy for your long work days."

I held my breath and waited for the expected speech on my long work hours, and the inevitable fight that would follow. "Okay."

Grady only shrugged. "Nothing else, that's it. Eat it, you'll like it."

He didn't push or cajole, and I appreciated that. It was unexpectedly sweet, and I felt the tears sting my eyes before they clouded my vision. "Sorry, don't mind me." I shook my head, feeling silly at the tears that started to fall.

"If you don't like it, you can just tell me," he said sounding slightly panicked. "Don't eat it and cry about it."

I smiled. "It's not that, it's just that this was a very sweet gesture. Thank you Grady."

He frowned and looked utterly confused. "Oh. Okay. You're welcome, I guess."

I felt his gaze on me as I devoured the burrito with animalistic vigor, savoring the sweet and spicy flavor of the meat, the texture of the rice and the green taste of the spinach. It wasn't what I would have chosen, but the salsa brought it all together even if there was no cheese or sour cream. "Delicious."

He nodded, seemingly satisfied with that one word compliment. "Look Margot, I meant what I said the other day. You might not be thrilled that you got pregnant by a lowly bartender, but I won't hide from this or run from my responsibility. This moral dilemma, or shame or whatever the hell it is, it's yours, not mine. I'm here, and I plan to be here for whatever you need. However you need me."

I stared at him for a long time, watched the way his jaw clenched and the blue in his eyes shifted from royal to sky blue.

"What?"

"Nothing, it's just I don't think I've heard you speak so many words at once."

His lips tugged into an amused grin. "Funny."

His words filtered through the tension and I blinked rapidly, knowing I needed to clear up this misunderstanding. "I'm not ashamed that I'm pregnant, least of all by you Grady."

He frowned and folded those massive arms. "So what is the problem then? Talk to me Margot."

I sighed, because the truth wasn't easy, and I didn't exactly feel comfortable admitting my failings to Grady of all people. "I'm too old to have a one night stand, never mind *unsafe* casual sex. It's embarrassing." I covered my face with both hands and shook my head. "I replayed that night and neither one of us, not once, even spared a thought to protection."

Grady nodded. "I'll admit that I was too busy wanting to get my hands and mouth on you to think about anything but your body, naked. But as for the rest of the world, for all they know, the condom broke. Or my swimmers are Olympians. Anything. People get pregnant all the time, and in a town like this, what people don't know they will make up."

"And that's the problem. What they're making up makes me look awful, and worse, silly."

"It's none of their damn business Margot."

I frowned at his words. "You don't care if people talk about you? About us?"

He laughed. "Hell no. Not unless they plan to get up for feedings, save for college, have the birds and the bees talk, or whatever else we have to do to get this kid from infancy to adulthood. Their opinion means less than nothing to me, and it shouldn't mean anything to you either."

He was right, people would talk no matter what. Even

once the truth was revealed, they would say what they wanted and believe whatever made the best story. "Thank you for that Grady. Your perspective is refreshing."

"It's realistic. When I first came to town people whispered about me behind my back, and even to my face. They speculated on everything from me being a fresh out of prison ex-con, in the witness protection program, and even a spy on the run."

"A spy! I hadn't heard that one, but yeah, that's a good story. Not as good as the lottery winner making his own slice of heaven."

"See? One hot night together and you get the baby you always wanted, and I get a kid I didn't even know I wanted." He shrugged. "It's better than anything they could make up, and they don't even know it, so it's like our little secret."

I grinned. "You're an optimist," I said with a sigh. "Another thing I didn't know about you."

"I'm a pragmatist," he said with a smile as he got to his feet. "And we have months and years to get to know more about each other Margot."

"I suppose you're right about that." It was odd, to think that a man I wasn't in a relationship with in any way, would without a doubt be in my life forever.

"Enjoy your lunch Margot, and if you need anything, food cravings, a shoulder to cry on, someone to bitch about your friends to, I am your first call."

It would take some getting used to, but I wanted to get

this right, to find a working co-parenting relationship with this man. "Okay Grady. I'm going to do my best. I promise."

He smiled and my heart stopped beating in my chest. It was wide and genuine, and so white it nearly blinded me. "That's all I'm asking. Take it easy."

I'm not ashamed to admit that I watched his tight backside and long muscular legs until they disappeared from view. And then I caught a few more seconds when I peeked out the window at his retreating form.

The man was hell on a woman's libido, and mine was now working overtime.

CHAPTER 14
GRADY

"Is there a special lady in your life big brother?" My sister Beth's laugh sounded light and airy on the other side of the video call, her smile was bright and I smiled in return.

"Is there someone special in *your* life," I rolled my eyes and shot back, sure that would get her off my case, at least for a moment or two.

But my sister was like a dog with a bone, or more specifically, a bloodhound on the scent. Somehow. "There are several someone's actually, now answer my question! Who is she?"

"It's not like that." I shook my head, because there was no way to explain my situation with Margot to my little sister, especially to mention a baby when I haven't told our mama yet.

Beth barked out a laugh. "So there *is* someone! Wait

until Mama hears, she'll be so thrilled. You know she thinks you're hiding from the world in that small town, don't you?"

"I'm aware, mostly because every time I offer to get her a ticket to come for a visit she comes up an excuse like bear season, or country bumpkins attacking." I laughed and shook my head. "She's just afraid of living in the country."

Beth laughed again. "Which is funny since Atlanta is far more dangerous than Carson Creek."

"Yeah, but it's a danger she knows, and now that she's living in the 'burbs I'm pretty sure she's forgotten danger is even a thing." Except for bumpkins and bears. "So how's business?"

"Checking up on your investment?" Her question was cheeky and playful, because that wasn't quite the truth.

"It's only my investment because you refused to take the place straight up."

"It's too much, Grady. Like I told you, when I can, I will purchase your share of the business and not a minute later. Besides, I kind of like us being business partners."

I was the definition of a silent partner, only offering help when it was requested. "So, working on anything interesting?"

"Oh yeah. A forest green 1969 Stingray is sitting on the bay, and I can't wait to get my hands on it. It needs a full overhaul under the hood, new leather interior and a few coats of paint, but she's a beauty."

"Send me photos?"

"Every step of the way," she promised. "How goes the bar business?"

"Booming as always," I told her and then launched into an explanation about the divorce parties. "I didn't know it was a thing, but they're serious money makers."

"Only you would find a way to cash in on divorce without going to law school Grady."

I shrugged. "What can I say? It's a talent."

"Don't give me that *aww shucks* shrug. It may work on the ladies of Carson Creek, but it doesn't work on me, mister."

I shrugged again. "I have no idea what you're talking about, Bethy."

"Don't call me that," she growled but her smile ruined the effect. "So tell me about this woman of yours."

"She's not my woman, and it's crazy complicated."

"Which means you're not ready to talk about it yet."

"Got it in one." Things with Margot were beyond complicated, but no matter how difficult she made it, I was determined to see this through. "You plan on visiting me anytime soon?"

"Oh yeah," she said sarcastically. "As soon as all these incredible classic cars stop winding up in my bay for ridiculous sums of money. You could come to me."

"Maybe I will." Visiting Beth would mean a quick trip to see my mama and then I could tell her, in person, that she was about to be a grandmother. The doorbell rang and

I frowned because I hadn't ordered any food, and the few guys I considered friends wouldn't stop by without calling first. "Hang on Beth."

"Don't mute it, I want to hear your small town life!"

I grunted, but said nothing as I made my way to the door and yanked it open without looking first because this was Carson Creek and the worst I would find is a drunk patron wanting a drink. "Margot. Is everything all right?"

"Fine," she said and smiled. "But after our last conversation I felt the need to make sure we were on the same page."

I stood stock-still, frozen for a quick moment before I remembered myself and waved her inside. "Same page?"

She nodded and stepped in. "I want to apologize to you for being such a bitch, but I had to be, which isn't really the point. Anyway," she sighed and shook her head. "This isn't about being ashamed of you Grady. I know I come off a little snobbish, but I'm not that bad, I promise. It's just, do you know what it's like to be a woman on the brink of fifty who got pregnant by a man half her age."

"Half? I'm over thirty Margot."

She nodded and waved dismissively in my direction. "Yes, thirty-two, I remember. Still, that's a big age difference."

"And again, it's nobody's damn business but ours. Why do you care so much what people think? If they are truly your friends they will be happy for you, no matter how it happened."

"Grady," she sighed.

"Margot who cares if you're a cougar?"

"Cougar?" Her voice was high-pitched and full of outrage. "Did you just call me a cougar?"

"You said it yourself, you threw yourself at a man half your age." I smiled as her face reddened and she fisted her hands at her hips.

"I said no such thing!"

"Wait. Shut the front door," Beth's voice sounded from the phone at my side. "You got a hot older chick pregnant? I gotta see her, lift the phone up so I can get a peek."

My jaw clenched in irritation. "Beth, now isn't a good time."

"Clearly," she laughed. "But lift the phone so I can get an intro and a look at her, and then I'll let you go handle the complicated cougar."

"I am *not* a cougar!" Margot roared again.

I closed my eyes and reached for patience as I lifted up the phone and pointed it at Margot. "Margot this is my annoying little sister Beth. Beth this is Margot."

"Hello Margot of the complicated cougar variety. It's nice to meet you."

Margot froze and then she smiled. "Hello Beth, who likes to fix classic cars. It's nice to meet you too. You don't look how I pictured."

"Expecting short spiky hair, and strong lesbian vibes?"

"I don't know, maybe? I wasn't expecting a beautiful woman with a grease stain on her nose."

"Oh Mama's gonna like you. Mama's gonna love her Grady. Oh shit, have you told Mama yet?"

"No," I growled. "This is all kind of new Bethy, and I have to go. Talk soon."

"Better talk to Mama soon, you know I'm crap at keeping secrets."

"Worse than crap," I growled. "I will do it, and soon. Just put her off if you can, yeah?"

"It's gonna cost you a visit and that's my final price," she said and ended the call.

I pinched the bridge of my nose and sighed as my life grew more complicated by the second.

"She's fun," Margot said with a smile in her tone.

"Yeah, a real riot. Come on in and have a seat. Are you hungry? Thirsty?"

"Yes," she answered. "To both. Please." The smile she flashed was sweet with a hint of sexy, and dammit my body responded.

I nodded and went to the kitchen to grab a tall glass of lemonade and returned with it. "What kind of hungry are you?"

She frowned and eyed the glass like it might bite her. "This is fine for now. Thank you."

I nodded and dropped down on the sofa beside her. "I don't want your apology Margot, just please remember that I exist and want to be a part of our kid's life."

"I'm trying, but I need you to know that if I fail, it's not because I think less of you, it's just because I'm used to handling life on my own."

"Same," I grunted. "We both have until that kid comes out to learn to do better at collaborating."

She laughed. "Collaborating?"

"Sounds better than the alternatives."

"The mushy emotional alternatives?"

I smiled. "Exactly." Our gazes locked together like puzzle pieces, and the air between us heated up and charged with electricity. My smile faded slowly and so did Margot's, until we just sat there and stared at one another, similar to teenagers in the midst of figuring out their attraction.

I don't know who leaned in first, or who's lips touched first, or who's tongue reached out first. Just as suddenly we were kissing, at first with our bodies as far a part as could be, while still being close enough to kiss. It was like we both knew that if we got any closer, that this chemistry between us, the combustible energy that had forever linked us, would explode again. If it did, things would become too complicated, and they were complicated enough.

I pulled back and stared at her violet eyes, searching for any sign that this wasn't what she wanted, that Margot felt taken advantage of, or caught off guard.

"Please, Grady," she moaned, and I was lost.

Any hope of being the good guy, of walking away from this moment, had gone up in smoke. Before I could think better of it, my hands were on her hips and pulling her onto my lap so the heat between her thighs surrounded my cock, suffused my entire lower body with heat. I growled and cupped her face gently before I lowered her mouth to mine and swiped my tongue across the seam of her lips.

Margot moaned and sank into me, engulfing me with her fire as she gripped my jaws and devoured my mouth. She kissed me like my mouth was the one she'd been waiting for. She played me like an electric guitar, and I let her, gripping her hips while she had her way with me.

My hands moved from her hips up to her small waist, and up even further before I cupped her lush breasts and she leaned into me. My thumb and forefinger found her hard nipple through her dress and bra, and she groaned. My cock twitched and Margot moaned again.

"Grady, stop teasing me. Please."

I smiled against her lips and kissed her deeply before I pulled back. "The teasing has just begun." Before she could ask what I was talking about, I gripped the hem of her silky blouse and pulled it up and over her head. The sight that greeted me was a beautiful lavender bra that held her breasts up and out, and I licked her sensitive flesh along the scalloped lace while she squirmed and made erotic noises.

Finally the bra was gone and my gaze feasted on her tits for a few seconds before my mouth honed in on her stiff peaks again. She was as soft and sweet as I remembered. Her flesh was silky soft and smooth, her nipples so hard that my mouth watered as I swiped my tongue along one hard nub and then the other. She arched into me, and I tasted every inch of her from the hard tips to the warm underside of her heavy breasts before I kissed my way up to her mouth.

"Grady, yes!"

The sound of my name on her lips, uttered in ecstasy instead of distaste, had my cock so hard I was sure the zipper would leave an imprint on it. My hips thrust up and she let out a guttural growl that I swallowed whole. "Margot."

She didn't answer, because her hands were busy with the button and zipper on my jeans and her mouth kissed and licked a swath of heat across my jaw. When she reached inside my jeans I was sure I would lose my mind and my load in one fell swoop. She shimmied off my lap and down to her knees, and the sight of her on her knees with my cock in her hands and a heated look on her face was the most beautiful fucking sight I had ever seen.

"Margot," I growled. "Not now."

She frowned and looked up at me. "What's wrong?"

"Nothing, except I'm hanging on by a thread here babe, and if you put those pretty lips on my cock this will be over before it gets started. Come here, just wrap me in your wet heat."

Her cheeks flamed, but she let me help her to her feet and out of her slacks and the panties that matched her bra. "If you insist," she said primly and my cock responded with a quick jerk.

"I do," I bit out and gripped her hips as she settled on top of me while I stroked my cock, unable to think of anything but being buried inside this woman. "Ah fuck, Margot."

She flashed a satisfied smile as she sank down onto me with a feral sound that was so out of the ordinary for her that my cock grew even harder. "You're so hard," she moaned. "And thick."

I held her hips but I let Margot set the pace, and she started slow. Achingly slow and I gritted my teeth to keep from thrusting up, from burying myself as deep as I could get. Her moves were slow and deliberate, up and down for long seconds at a time.

And then her legs shook and started to buckle.

My grip tightened on her hips and I moved her up and down on my cock while her fingers dug into my shoulders. "Grady," she moaned as her movements became frantic, and I fought to keep a hold of her as she chased her pleasure. "Yes," she whispered in my ear.

Control snapped and I was on my feet as my gaze swept the room in search of the perfect spot. I found a bare spot of wall and pressed her against it as I continued to thrust deeper and harder into her tight, wet core.

Margot's cries grew louder and more demanding, and I was determined to give her exactly what she wanted. "Oh shit," she growled and that's when the last of my control snapped.

Knowing I was the one who made Miss Prim & Proper slip up and utter an expletive gave me a boost I didn't need. I kissed her neck and collarbone while my hips pounded up into her and she began to clutch and pulse around me. She was close, and so was I, our pleasure was imminent. "Margot," I growled.

Her response was to dig her heels into my ass and I pressed my chest to hers, thrusting harder and deeper until we both fell over the edge. Together. Her body went slack immediately even as she continued to pulse around me, prolonging my pleasure until my own legs started to wobble. She pulled back with a surprised smile.

"You all right?"

"No," I grunted. "I'm pretty sure you've milked me dry, nymph."

"Me?" Margot shook her head with a sweet, shy smile. "You must have me confused with someone else."

"I don't see any other hot as fuck businesswomen squeezing my cock dry. Do you?" She clenched around me harder and I growled. "Upstairs," I said even though my feet were already on the move and seconds later we collapsed into bed. My bed.

"You don't have to call me hot."

I frowned at her, still panting from her orgasm. "Why wouldn't I? It's your mouth I have a problem with, not the way you look." I fell back against the bed. "Oh fuck, don't tell me you also don't know you're hot as shit?"

Her face turned impossibly pinker. "I'm not."

"You are, Margot. Great tits, long legs, lush lips, violet eyes and those prim dresses that make me wonder what's underneath? Yeah, you're fucking hot."

"Grady," she sighed.

"What? You want me to tell you that I've fantasized about you sucking me off, because then I get to fuck you without hearing your stuck up comments?"

She gasped. "Must you be so crude?"

"In this moment, hell yeah I do." This woman was crazy. "You know you're the shit when it comes to business or social status, but you look at yourself every day and you're not sure that you're beautiful? Makes no fucking sense to me."

"Grady, stop."

"No." I rolled over until I was half on top of her with my fingers between her legs. "How about this, I'll make you come until you tell me you believe you're beautiful."

She shook her head. "I can't."

"Wanna bet?" I rubbed her swollen clit and her hips bucked off the bed. "Yeah, get ready Margot. I need you to know you're the shit, so our baby knows he or she is the shit. Got it?"

She nodded and when I slipped one finger deep inside of her, she spread her legs and rolled her hips, practically begging me for more. "Yes," she panted.

"Good. Now lie back and show me how much you like it."

Almost immediately she grabbed my wrist, and I added a second finger to her heat, pumping hard and deep until Margot lost her mind and her icy cool demeanor.

"Okay, I don't think I have another one in me," she said around short, shallow breaths.

I smiled and kissed her lips. "I guess that means you're ready to tell me how hot you are?"

"Grady," she whined.

"Guess we're not done yet."

CHAPTER 15
MARGOT

"We really should stop meeting like this."

My words were breathless and well satisfied. *Very* well satisfied, but they were also true. For more than a week now Grady and I have been burning up the sheets. At his place as well as mine, and even once in his office at the bar.

It was becoming a problem. A big orgasmic problem.

Okay, the orgasms weren't the problem, not really, it was just that everything else about the person giving me the orgasms was the problem.

Grady ran one finger along the length of my spine. Up and down, up and down, in a slow drugging motion that had my eyelids growing heavy and my body sank even deeper into his soft, comfortable bed.

"I didn't start this sweetheart, you did."

My eyelids fluttered to fight sleep as I looked up at Grady. "So now I'm a sweetheart?"

He nodded confidently. "You're naked in my bed and smelling like me, so hell yeah, you're *sweetheart* now honey." Just to make his point, he winked and I felt my body respond. "What's the problem? You're a wildfire in the sheets, and I'm the perfect person to indulge your carnal needs."

I bit back a laugh. "My carnal needs? So you're saying that you're just helping me out and get nothing out of it."

Grady sighed and fell backwards against the bed. "Clearly that's exactly what I'm saying," he answered with a healthy dose of sarcasm. "Obviously I think you're hot, or we wouldn't be here. Hot and horny for me? Well that's just an irresistible combination that no man can resist."

Hot and horny.

That made me sound like a sexy twentysomething who just can't get enough, which *would* be hot. But I wasn't any of that. I was...hell I don't know what I was. "Irresistible even when I'm fat and bloated?"

He laughed. "When you get fat and bloated, come and find me and maybe I'll have an answer for you, Margot."

When he said my name like that, half exasperated and half filled with affection, I didn't know how to respond. I didn't know what to think or how to feel. It was the tone of two people who had been together for a long time, who were comfortable with each other. Not two people accidentally bound together for life. "Now is when I'm fat and bloated." I turned over and pointed at my belly and my thighs.

"Pregnant," he amended. "I see that you are pregnant, and I can barely even notice until I get my hands on you." To hammer his point home Grady put one large hand on my stomach that already showed signs of the life growing inside, and rubbed it gently. "You look at this and you see fat, but all I see is signs of our baby growing things like fingers and toes and belly buttons."

"Belly buttons?" I choked on a laugh. "How many do you think kids have?"

Grady shrugged. "Just making a point. You're not fat Margot, there's just another human growing inside of you." He rubbed my belly almost reverently, and I had to blink back tears at the sweetness of his words and actions.

"If you say so."

"I do," he growled and rolled off the bed with ease.

I blinked when he held a hand out to me. "Kicking me out?"

He smiled. "No. Shower. It's humid even with the cool night air. We'll both sleep better after a shower."

My mind instantly went to shower sex, because I couldn't remember ever having sex in the shower in my life, which was really a sad state of affairs for a woman nearing fifty. "I doubt either of us will sleep much after showering together."

His mouth curled into an even bigger grin. "We'll see about that. Come on."

I put my hand in his, it was big and warm and strong, comforting in a way I hadn't expected with my heart still racing from the last orgasm, my nipples still hard and breast still aching. I looked around the now familiar bathroom and grinned. It was nice and masculine, but without any of the flourishes in my bathroom such as decorative soaps and unnecessary towels. A week of nonstop sex with the father of my unborn child, and I didn't hate the differences between us as much.

"You're thinking too hard. Warm or hot?" His blue eyes stared at up at me, one hand gripped the shower lever perched between hot and warm.

"Hot," I answered with a smile. "As hot as you can stand it."

Grady smiled with approval and cranked the handle until it was almost as hot as it could get. "A woman after my own heart."

My heart sped up at his words and I needed to remind myself that we didn't hate each other anymore, if it was ever hate at all, but that didn't mean we were turning into something. We weren't, we were just two people getting to know each other because we had no choice in the matter. "All of these compliments and I might start to think you actually like me Grady."

"I do," he said simply and took a step back to wave me in. "Ladies first."

I groaned as soon as the water hit my skin. It was hot and steamy and I could barely see Grady when he stepped in beside me, but he was so much man I could *feel* him even though he hadn't touched me. Yet. The spray was perfect, and I turned to let the beads of water throttle my back.

"Feel good?"

"Oh yeah," I moaned and let my head fall back under the shower spray. "Oh!" More water rained down from the ceiling and shocked a laugh out of me. "That's a nice touch," I told him and closed my eyes.

"No, this is a nice touch," he said and his big hands began to roam my body. I came alive at his touch, the way he cupped my breasts as if they were some treasure instead of a sign I needed to drop a few pounds. His hands lingered and when I opened my eyes I saw traces of soapy bubbles and gasped. He was actually washing me.

"Is this all right?"

Was it? I nodded, and he continued his task at hand, rubbing his hands in circles around my breasts and then down my waist before he pressed his chest to mine and let his hands slide down my back easily thanks to the ocean scented body wash. He lingered on my butt and instead of feeling self-conscious I moaned at the unexpected pleasure. Who knew the butt was an erogenous zone? Or maybe it was the big wall of hot man pressed up against me. "My turn."

"Not yet," he growled and stepped back to squat down where he lathered up more soap and used both hands on my right leg and then my left. And then he did it again.

And again. I trembled with need by the time his hands slid up the inside of my thighs and found me wet and swollen. Grady groaned and slid one finger back and forth across my seam until his thick finger breached it and hit my clit. Fireworks lit behind my eyes, but all I could see was Grady and the way he looked at me, as if I was a gift just for him.

"Grady," I growled and he stopped as hot water ran down my skin in a perfect light massage. And then his mouth was there, French kissing me while my thighs trembled with the effort to keep me upright. His tongue flicked against my clit over and over, and my body shook with desire, with impending pleasure. "Grady," I moaned again, and waited for him to slide a finger inside of me, or better yet, to stand up and slide into me, but he did none of that. He used his lips and his tongue—and oh my!—even his teeth to bring me to orgasm. My legs shook, but Grady held me close and his tongue never stopped moving, not even when I begged him to stop.

Grady looked up at me with a smile in his blue eyes and gave me one final, achingly slow lick.

My body floated until I finally came back to earth with a wide grin. "Wow," I panted. "Shower sex, and an oral orgasm. Are you magic?"

Grady laughed as he stood and switched our positions so he was under the water. "I don't know, am I?" He reached out to me when my legs threatened to buckle and pulled me close.

"You just might be." I placed my hands on his shoulders and slid them down over his chest and his abs, everywhere but the huge throbbing cock that was literally between us. "And this is your magic wand."

He laughed, and it was beautiful, it echoed in the bathroom, the rich sound put a smile on my face as I reached for the soap and took my time exploring every inch of his big, strong body. He had muscles everywhere which only made me more curious about his life before he won the lottery and moved to Carson Creek.

Not now, I told myself, determined to live in this exact moment right here. I didn't need to worry about the future, or work, or anything else except this man who seemed to be under my spell.

My hand found him long and hard and one tug pulled an erotic growl from him. "Margot."

I blinked up at him and smiled. "Yes, Grady?"

Instead of speaking he gripped my hand which stopped my movements as the water poured over us, and then he slammed the water off. In the next breath he had me in his arms and marched us both, soaking wet, from the bathroom. He went back for an oversized navy blue towel and haphazardly dried me off and then him.

I crawled onto the bed, unsure what had just happened, because the air in the room changed, it shifted into something intense that vibrated my body with need. The moment he lay beside me, I pounced and used my hands and my mouth to explore him all over again.

I was transfixed, mesmerized by the sounds I drew

from him. They were the grunts and growls I'd grown familiar with over the months, but they were different, filled with heat and desire, and an urgency that sped up my own pulse. I wanted him, badly, but more than that, I wanted to please him, and show him that this wasn't all about me.

His hips bucked when my lips closed around his erection, and he let out a long, low growl of pleasure as my lips slid down to the base. I repeated the move, slow and drawn out, over and over until his hands fisted in my hair and his sounds became nothing more than grunts and moans.

It was an out of body experience for me, the urgent need I felt to please this man, to hear the erotic sounds he made over and over. I was like a woman on a mission, and that mission was to make him scream my name. It wasn't something I'd ever experienced before, that primal need to claim a man in the bedroom, but right now it was all I wanted.

I gripped him with one hand and sped up my movements and Grady rewarded me with another growl and his hands tightened in my hair. His hips moved in slow, unconscious strokes that told me I was doing everything right, and when I felt his cock grow harder in my hands and his sack tighten, I knew he was close. "Margot," he grunted. "Fuck, yes."

It wasn't a scream, but it was a nice start ,and I took him a little deeper and gave him a little more tongue.

"Shit Margot, babe. I'm...oh fuck." His body went tense and all movement stopped for a long moment and I took advantage of the moment to take him even deeper. And then I swallowed. "Fuck, babe!" His body started to move again, to shake and convulse as pleasure worked its way to the surface and he exploded underneath me.

I watched and it was a beautiful sight, Grady with his eyes squeezed tight as pleasure flowed from him, his big, strong capable body totally under my command. "Wow."

Long seconds later Grady looked down at me. "What?"

"I never knew it would be such a turn-on to make a man do all that," I said and motioned to him.

"Yeah?"

I nodded.

Grady smiled and crooked a finger at me. "Let's see what else you can make me do."

My eyes widened and I crawled up the bed, exhausted but eager to see what else Grady had in store. He gifted me with another orgasm I would never forget, and then he did something totally unexpected, wrapped me in his arms and tucked his chin over my shoulder, and fell asleep.

It was a cuddle. Even better—and more confusing—it was an after sex cuddle, which almost made this feel real.

It's not real, I reminded myself just moments before I drifted off to sleep.

To prove my point, the bed was empty and cold when I woke up the next morning. I gathered the few items of clothes I could find and dressed quickly, determined to make my way to the exit without feeling like a woman doing a walk of shame.

"Going somewhere?"

Grady's deep voice startled a squeak out of me, and I turned around and nearly swallowed my tongue at the sight of him. Grady wore nothing but a pair of black pants that hung low on his hips, showing off that sexy vee I'd spent a little too much time on last night, and all the colors of his tattoos.

"I, um...yeah?"

His lips twitched as if he knew what I was thinking and what I was doing, but he didn't call me out on it. "Come have something to eat before you go." Without waiting to see if I was agreeable to his offer of breakfast, he turned and disappeared into the kitchen.

Since the rest of my clothes hadn't magically appeared, I followed him into the kitchen. "Smells delicious." I watched the muscles in his back move as he took food from the stove and counter to the kitchen table.

"Have a seat."

I obeyed without question and took a seat as Grady set a tall glass of sparkling amber liquid in front of me. "Ginger ale?"

He nodded as if this act of kindness was no big deal. "You said your nausea is worse in the mornings so I got some for you."

I blinked rapidly because the tears were imminent, but

a few drops slipped out before I could catch them. "Grady," I squeaked.

He froze. "It's not your brand? There were only two in the supermarket, and I went for the fancy kind made with real ginger."

I shook my head. "No, it's perfect. It's really thoughtful. Thank you."

"If you cry over ginger ale, wait until you see breakfast," he grinned arrogantly and set a plate in front of me piled high with food. "Shallot and spinach scrambled omelet with cheese. Buttered toast. Berry salad. Eat up," he ordered and took the seat beside me.

We ate in silence like this was an everyday part of our routine, having breakfast together.

The scarier part was that I didn't hate the idea. Not even a little bit.

In fact, I didn't hate it at all.

CHAPTER 16
GRADY

Payroll was the bane of my existence, but it was a necessary evil because employees expected to be paid. But the stupid software didn't care, as evidenced by the half a dozen glitches in the first five minutes of the task.

"I should have done it daily," I grumbled to myself the same way I did every single week. The system appreciated daily use, but adding in a week's worth of shifts at once seemed to piss it off.

My phone rang and I reached for it without thinking, because anything, or anyone would be better than payroll. "Hello," I barked into the phone.

"That is how you answer your mama's call is it?"

I smiled at her thick Georgia accent and shrugged even though she couldn't see me. "Didn't know it was you Mama. How are you?"

"Fine. Is payroll gettin' the best of you again?"

I laughed. "How did you know?"

"Mama knows," was her only answer. "How's life in your teeny tiny town?"

"It's great Mama, which you would know if you ever came for a visit. How's life in Georgia?"

"Quiet and peaceful, and surprisingly active." She laughed and caught me up on every little detail of the lives of people I've never met. "I baked six dozen cookies for the elementary school bake sale, started a knitting circle that's now turned into a dirty books and cocktails club, with some knitting thrown in," she laughed. "It's wonderful."

I smiled, happy to see her settling into her new life. "I'm glad to hear that Mama. If that's the stuff you like, you will definitely love visiting Carson Creek."

"They put you on the welcoming committee, or do you all get some type of bonus for recruiting new residents?" Mama laughed at her own joke and I joined her even though it was at my expense.

"Are you becoming a stand-up comic for your second act?"

"Now who's the funny man?" She laughed again and it faded to a wistful sort of happy. "I miss you Grady."

"I miss you too Mama. I hope to make time for a visit before summer is over," I told her honestly. It wasn't that I couldn't get away, it was a matter of trusting my bar to someone else.

"Are you comin' up to tell me about the woman you

knocked up in person?" Mama laughed as the silence went on and on, and dammit, even though I knew she was about to lay into me, I still missed her.

"Dammit Beth," I growled.

"Don't go blamin' your sister. It's your own fault for telling that girl anything when she can't even hold water, never mind a secret as big as this."

"It's not a secret, and I didn't tell her. We were on the phone when Margot showed up at my place and I forgot about Beth."

Mama didn't say anything for a long time, and then she let out an indecipherable huff. "Margot, huh? Sounds fancy. Does she spell it with an 'aux' too?"

"No," I growled. "You have no idea how fancy this one is."

"I have some idea, you always did like the fancy girls. But more importantly, are things serious with you and this Margot?"

"No. It's less than that, we barely even like each other." That wasn't entirely true anymore. Over the past couple weeks we had become more than enemies, hell more than even frenemies. When we were alone and naked together we seemed to get on just fine.

Mama snorted, and I could almost picture her shaking her head. "You liked each other well enough to make a baby."

"It's complicated. She's a little older and a whole lot snooty." And that was putting it mildly.

Mama laughed again, this laugh was a flat out guffaw. "You always did like your women a little bit stuck up."

"That's not true!" I liked my women simple and easy-going, sought them out for that exact reason.

"Anita Whittaker," she reminded me of a girl I crushed on junior year. "She was a judge's daughter wasn't she? Thought she was at the top of the food chain."

I nodded. "Yeah okay, there was Anita."

"Amanda Rochester," she tossed out another name, her voice full of mischief. "Didn't she and her family spend summers in France?"

"Okay, okay I take your point, but I was a kid and they were hot, which was pretty much my only criteria back then. Margot is different," I told her and tried to explain the class difference and the way Margot was.

"Sounds like tugging pigtails and tripping in the hall."

"Excuse me?"

"You know how kids mistreat each other to hide their true feelings? Sounds like what you two were doing until you fell into bed together."

"She's beautiful, but judgmental, but lately she hasn't been," I admitted more to myself than to her.

"So I'm right. This is an extreme way to get me to visit, but effective," she admitted.

"Well," I sighed. "If you would just visit, such extremes wouldn't be necessary."

She laughed again and the sound was welcome. "So

what's happening, you're having a baby together, but you're not together?"

I thought of the last few weeks with Margot. The first week was a nonstop sex-a-thon, but then shifted into something more like friends with benefits, but the emphasis was on friends and benefits, separately, which made it what? "It's complicated."

"You're still sleeping together," she guessed correctly. "And now things are getting confusing?"

"Yeah," I admitted. "I like her, and she seems to like me, but that's not enough to get over a year of sniping at each other, is it?"

"You're askin' the wrong question, my boy. You two are having a baby together, isn't that enough to put the past behind you?"

"It has been so far."

"Then you're off to a good start."

"Hang on Mama, someone's at the door. Come in."

"Hey, you have a visitor." My part-time worker peeked her head inside the office.

"Send them in," I told her and turned my focus back to my call. "I need to get to work and finish the payroll. Let's talk soon about that visit yeah?"

"Sure thing, honey. I love you."

"Love you too, Mama." The door opened just as I set the phone down and Margot strolled in wearing a figure hugging green dress that made my dick stand on edge. "Margot. Hi."

"Hey," she smiled. "Are you busy?"

"You mean other than this payroll software kicking my ass and my mama giving me a hard time? Nope, free as a bird."

She grinned. "Well I'll keep this quick. I have a doctor's appointment on the ninth of next month, and I wondered if you wanted to go, you know to be there?"

Her words shocked me into silence. "You mean for the baby?"

She nodded and flashed a wide grin. "Exactly that. Unless you wanted to come to other doctor visits with me?"

"No. I mean, yeah I would love to go. Thanks." She stared at me with a hint of amusement on her face, like she was trying not to laugh at me. "Are you hungry?"

"You don't always have to feed me Grady."

"I know, but I want to feed you. It's something I'm good at, and it directly helps you and the baby. So?"

She shook her head. "I had a fruit and nut salad with yogurt for lunch, and for breakfast Pippa brought a terrifying green drink that was surprisingly delicious. Happy?"

"Thrilled." I fell back against my chair and let out a long breath. "Mama knows. Beth let it slip, because of course she did."

Margot stiffened. "And? Was she angry? Upset? Does she think I'm robbing the cradle?"

I barked out a laugh. "No. She asked a ton of questions,

most of which I don't have answers to, but she's planning to come for a visit. Finally."

"To curse me out?"

"No, to meet you would be my guess. And to get a good look at the town she thinks is straight out of a horror movie."

Her violet eyes widened. "Your mother watches horror movies?"

"Oh yeah. All of them, no matter how bad or how cheesy, she loves them all. She will ask you about your favorite and least favorite horror movie, so be prepared."

Margot looked terrified as she nodded. "I'll um, keep that in mind. Do you know when?"

"Nah, but you will be the first to know. After Mama, of course."

"Of course." She nodded. "All right then I guess I'll see you around?"

I nodded. "Tomorrow night for dinner. I'm going to cook, well more accurately, I'm going to throw some red meat on the grill. How does that sound?"

"Deliciously masculine. Should I bring anything?"

I gave her a long, assessing look and licked my lips. "You are more than enough Margot."

Surprise flashed in her eyes and she nodded, and then bolted out the door.

CHAPTER 17
MARGOT

Arriving late to an event because my morning sickness had decided to stray into afternoon and evening was not how I preferred to arrive fashionably late.

As it was, Grady's Bar was filled with beautiful people from all facets of the music industry, and even the folks of Carson Creek got all gussied up to mix and mingle with the famous as well as the infamous. Meanwhile I showed up in a belted green dress in an effort to hide my growing belly for just one night.

The bar looked great. It was the same old rustic local bar vibe, but Carlotta had done a fantastic job with decorating, and there were gold records dangling from the ceiling, cowgirls sauntered around with champagne and cocktails. It was all very cowboy chic, which I'd thought sounded rather cheap and cheesy, but Carlotta never failed when it came to giving clients exactly what they wanted, even if they didn't know what they wanted until they saw it.

"Margot, get on over here darlin'." Roman wore a wide grin, happy to be the man of the evening as the music world came together to celebrate his debut solo album release.

"Roman, you're looking like quite the tasty treat tonight."

"From you Margot, I will take that with the highest of honors." He smacked a flirty kiss to my cheek and whispered. "Pregnancy looks great on you."

"Thank you." I felt a blush flame my cheeks at his sweet words. "Congratulations on the album Roman. You're going to be an even bigger star than you are now."

He laughed and pointed at Derek and Ryan. "You mean I'll be bigger than these bozos, don't you?"

"Finally you get to be the center of attention is more like it," Derek growled and wrapped an arm around Bella. "As if being the baby didn't make you center of the universe."

"Yeah, but now I get to be center of the universe for millions of women. Millions," he added with emphasis.

The brothers' camaraderie was beautiful to witness, even if they spent most of their time apparently giving each other a hard time. "Congratulations again Roman, you deserve this and more." I made a quick escape just before a group of executives arrived to tell Roman how wonderful he was, heading to the bar to get something to combat this nausea that refused to go away.

Didn't this kid know that I had to work?

Grady turned the full attention of his blue gaze to me and studied me for so long I began to feel uneasy. "What's wrong?"

"Nothing," I sighed and instinctively put a hand to my head. "Do I look that terrible?"

"You look beautiful," he growled. "But not yourself. Sick or tired, or something." His gaze lingered again, like I was some fragile flower.

"I'm just tired, and yes, a little nauseous, but it's nothing to get all worked up about."

He nodded and slid a glass in my direction. "I'll just have a sparkling water," I told him.

"Yeah, with lemon," he shot back. "Drink."

I smiled at his bossy tone and obvious concern. Having Grady worry about me wasn't so bad and I felt warmth blossom in my belly. "Thank you, bossy pants."

"Me? Bossy pants? I must have learned from the best," he said with a small grin that told me he meant me.

"Yes well, as the OG bossy pants, I need to go mingle and make sure all is well." Even though this was Carlotta's event to put on, it was booked through me at The Old Country House, which meant I needed to make an appearance, to make sure everyone was having a good time.

"Don't overdo it," he shouted to my retreating back, and I waved a dismissive hand as I did my best to work the crowd while pushing my nausea down deep. The bar was packed and everyone was smiling, deep in conversation and the drinks were flowing. The night was going wonderfully and I would feel great about that, if every step I took didn't make my stomach flip.

"Margot!" I turned to see Carlotta waving me over to the table where she sat with Chase, a big colorful drink in front of her. "Come on and take a load off. You look exhausted."

I took the seat and sighed. "If one more person tells me that, I might develop a complex about it."

Chase snickered and Carlotta gave him a playful shove. "You look great, Margot. Really."

"Yes," Carlotta confirmed. "You absolutely do, but that has nothing to with how exhausted you look. Are you feeling all right?"

I nodded. "I'm feeling as tired as I apparently look." I shook my head at the thought that I wasted time on my hair and makeup when I looked so clearly old and haggard. "Worry about Roman and the party, this is just pregnancy. Apparently." It was the first time I admitted it out loud, and the record didn't scratch, the world didn't stop spinning. Everything just carried on as usual.

"Roman doesn't need me to worry about him," Carlotta laughed and motioned to where he stood in the middle of a large crowd, talking wildly with his hands. "He's enjoying being the belle of the ball."

"Happy clients are music to my ears."

"The studio is loving this low-key setting and all the photos of Roman with childhood friends in a local bar. They are positively thrilled, so don't worry about anything Margot, except maybe getting some food in your belly."

Just as the words left Carlotta's mouth, Pippa showed up at the table with two plates of food. "Margot you look like you're getting to be run down. I brought bread and spreads, veggies and dip and mini sandwiches. Eat it all. Please." She motioned for me to slide over, which I did, and dropped down beside me with the plates. "Eat. Now."

I laughed. "Since when did getting pregnant mean everyone gets to boss you around."

Pippa laughed. "Since forever, especially when you live in Carson Creek. Everyone told me what to eat, brought it to me, and sometimes they even watched me eat it. It was annoying and well-intentioned."

"Just like Carson Creek," we all said in unison and laughed.

"Thank you for the food," I told her with a sigh. "It seems my morning sickness has shifted to the all-day variety."

Pippa smiled in commiseration. "You're going to hate this suggestion, but I carried crackers with me in my purse and I kept a six pack of ginger ale in the trunk of my car just in case."

"I have them in my purse," I admitted sheepishly. "But my purse is in the car so it doesn't help me at the moment."

Ryan chose that moment to approach the table, probably to get some time with his wife. "Ginger ale and toasted bread, lightly buttered. From Grady," he said to me with a knowing smile.

"Well now, isn't that interesting," Pippa mused out loud.

"No. It's not even a little bit interesting," I said and grabbed a piece of bread and shoved it in my mouth with a smile. "Just Carson Creek helping each other out," I said around an obscenely large mouthful of food.

Things with Grady were confusing enough that I didn't want to add town speculation to the list of things I needed to worry about.

CHAPTER 18
GRADY

~August

"Are you ready for this?" It was strange that it was me asking Margot that question instead of the other way around, but after two days of bargaining she'd finally relented and let me pick her up for the doctor's appointment. Now we sat inside my car in the parking lot of the medical center in absolute silence.

Margot nodded, and then she shook her head. "I'm ready, but I'm terrified because now it's real."

I laughed and put a hand to her belly. "I hate to tell you this honey, but it's already real."

She smacked at my hand and laughed. "I know *that*, but this is different. You're here and there's no going back, not that I want to go back, but you know what I mean."

I nodded. "When I walk in there with you for this

appointment, it becomes official. I am your baby's daddy, and the whole town will know by end of business today."

She huffed out a bitter laugh. "They'll probably know before we make it back to the car, but yes. Exactly that." She sighed and shook her head. "It's just, I thought I was done with the gossip, but this will just start it up all over again."

"I don't think anything is going to stop the gossip Margot. This is the most interesting thing that's happened since that country singer was in town to record with Derek."

"You're not helping."

"Okay," I said and drew the word out into about four syllables before I jumped from the car and jogged around to the passenger side. "Let's go."

She blinked and her brows dipped in confusion. "You're kicking me out?"

"Yes. Out of the car and into that building, so we can find out how our little one is doing. No one is ever ready to be thrust into the spotlight, but this has to be done Margot. For the baby."

Those words seemed to be the magic trick to get her out of the vehicle, because she accepted my hand and I helped her from the car. I kept my hand on her lower back to guide her towards the door, inside the elevator and up to the seventh floor of the building where a full waiting room greeted us.

"This has to be a joke," she whispered.

I laughed because I knew what she meant. It was late afternoon and there was no way in hell all of these people could see the doctor before the offices closed. "Seems like it, but maybe they're just looking because you're the prettiest and most stylish pregnant woman in the room." I kissed her cheek, planted her in a chair and went to check in with the receptionist.

"Three o'clock for Margot Blanchard Devereaux."

The woman looked up at me and blinked. "And you are?"

I bit back the smart ass retort on the tip of my tongue. "I'm helping Margot today. Is there paperwork or anything she needs to fill out?"

The nosy receptionist typed on the computer and turned back to me. "No, she's all good." Then her eyes went wide. "Grady. The bartender."

I nodded. "I also own the place, but yeah, I'm the bartender."

"And you…" she started, but realized how inappropriate her next question might be and just let her gaze dart back and forth between where Margot sat and me. "Wow. Go Margot."

I laughed. "Thanks."

"Sorry," she said as a furious blush stained her neck and cheeks. "The doctor should be with you in the next five minutes or so."

"Thanks again," I told her and went to stand beside Margot. "How are you feeling?"

"Better than most mornings, but that only means I'll be sick for the rest of the day."

A woman with long black braids leaned forward and put a hand on Margot's. "Sorry to eavesdrop, but what you want to do is eat a big meal when you feel fine, regardless of the time of day." She turned her gaze to me. "If she's still feeling fine after this, take her out for a late lunch or early dinner. Doesn't make it go away completely, but curbs it considerably."

"Really?"

The woman nodded. "Worked for me with baby number two," she said proudly. "This one doesn't even give me a chance to eat anything. It's like the mere thought of food sends me running for the nearest toilet."

Margot looked horrified and the woman just smiled.

"It's why they're so cute, to make us forget all about the sore nipples, achy lady parts, of the lack of food for nine straight months." She laughed. "And we get to hold it over their heads for the rest of their lives."

At those words Margot relaxed and shared a laugh with the woman.

"Margot," the nurse called out with a wide smile. "Come on back." The nurse's eyes widened at the sight of me beside Margot and I leaned in with a grin.

"I think we were both wrong. Word's gonna get out before you even put on that paper gown."

A reluctant laugh spilled from Margot as we walked past the nurse. "It is what it is, I guess."

I stood back and tried to be as unobtrusive as possible while the nurse weighed Margot and took her vitals, and I diverted my gaze when she undressed even though I'd already seen and tasted every inch of her. "All good?"

She nodded. "I think I need your help getting on the table. It's made for giants."

"You're nervous," I told her and helped her onto the table. "What are you worried about specifically?"

"Nothing specific, but I'm nervous. Anxious."

"Just try to relax. Worrying about it now won't change what the doctor has to tell us, but it will increase your blood pressure which I've read isn't good for the baby."

"You've been reading about pregnancy?"

I nodded, smiled instead of being insulted at the surprise in her voice. "Of course. At fifteen weeks pregnant the baby is about the size of an apple, about fifty-five grams."

Margot gasped and shook her head just as the doctor knocked and stepped inside. "Good afternoon Margot... and friend?"

"Father," Margot offered up without a hint of unease or discomfort.

"Oh. Well, good afternoon mom and dad. Are we ready for our fifteen week checkup?"

Margot nodded and I did too, but I stepped back behind the inclined table to make sure I was out of the way as much as possible without leaving the room. "As ready as I can be. Today feels real, and I can't say why."

"Today you get to meet your baby. Well sort of," the young and bubbly doctor chirped in. "First, tell me how you've been feeling."

I listened carefully as Margot rattled off her symptoms, some of which were new to me. "But other than shifting from morning to the rest of the day. I'm feeling all right, other than terrified."

The doctor laughed and questioned Margot as she measured her belly and performed a quick internal exam. "Everything looks good. Are we ready to see the little angel?"

"We can *see* the baby?" It was a silly question, but I wasn't prepared for this.

"Well, see the baby in the digital sense. It has arms and legs and everything, but we won't be able to see it like a photo," she said and prepared a giant wand and some thick blue liquid. "Ready Mom?"

Margot nodded and I stepped forward to grip her hand. "I think so."

"It's just an image," I told her. "The baby isn't gonna start crying and demand you feed him or her."

"Funny," she snorted.

I went completely still at the throbbing through rushing water sound that filled the room. "What is that?"

The doctor smiled. "That is the heartbeat," she said and leaned forward to squint at the screen.

Margot's grip tightened on my hand and she tried to sit up. "Is something wrong? Something is wrong isn't it?

That sounds too fast and I'm too old, and it's all wrong isn't it."

I rubbed her shoulder in gentle circles and dropped a kiss on top of her head. "Doc, tell Margot she's wrong and that nothing's wrong."

Sympathy swam in the kind doctor's eyes. "He's right, which is something every father longs to hear," she laughed. "He's right though, nothing is wrong. And you're right, that heart beat does sound too fast. For one baby."

"What does that mean?" My gaze narrowed at the doctor as my growled question echoed in the room over the rapid beating of our baby's heart.

"It means that I would be very worried about that heartbeat if it were just one baby. But it's perfectly expected with twins."

"Twins!" We both shouted at the same time.

Nonplussed, the doctor smiled. "Yep. There's a heart here and another one right there. Look at the little black flutter," she instructed and pointed at the screen.

"That's the heart?" I asked in shocked.

"The hearts," she answered, pointing to a second flutter. "Two hearts."

"Holy shit. Twins." I smiled and looked down at Margot who stared at the screen with a terrified, half-blank expression. Her face never moved, not once throughout the rest of the appointment. She was in shock. "Say something," I implored her once we were settled back inside the car.

"I don't know what to say Grady."

"Okay," I started the engine and pulled out of the parking space. "That's enough to let me know you're all right. Just don't panic and we'll both be fine." I drove her straight to my house without another word and guided her inside. "Have a seat."

I knew things were bad when she nodded and dropped down on the sofa without arguing or telling me I was being too bossy.

I rushed up to the main bathroom and started a bath with the bubbles Beth sent because she thought it would be funny. I made my way back downstairs and into the kitchen for a cup of tea. "Come on."

She shook her head. "I'm not tired," she said and followed me up the stairs.

"Good, because I wouldn't want you to drown in the bath. Come on before the water gets cold."

She froze behind me. "You drew me a bath?"

"Yeah, I figured you needed to relax or decompress, or whatever. Here's some tea instead of, you know, champagne or wine."

She smiled. "Thank you Grady. This is incredibly sweet."

I nodded and left her alone, a t-shirt on the bed for her to change into afterwards, and made my way downstairs. The pregnant woman with the braids came to mind and her words of advice, and I made a beeline for the kitchen.

My mama cooked almost every night and made sure

both Beth and I knew how to feed ourselves properly for the fateful day when we moved out on our own. I didn't often cook at home, but I'd learned to enjoy it, and now that I had someone else to cook for I settled into the process of crushing tomatoes and chopping garlic and herbs.

The silence above me told me she must have fallen asleep, which was probably just what she needed, so I took my time in the kitchen, enjoying the novelty of making a meal in the middle of the day.

"It smells incredible in here." Margot's sweet voice sounded behind me and I turned to her with a smile. "What are you cooking?"

"My famous chicken riggies, of course."

"Of course," she joked. "What the hell is a riggie?"

"It's a rigatoni. Spicy chicken rigatoni, but not too spicy because you're pregnant."

"Am I?"

"Funny. Did you have a good nap?" She was sexy and adorable in my oversized t-shirt, her hair half dry and wavy as it stuck up all around her head. Her legs looked long even though my shirt hung down to her knees.

"I did. Thank you for the bath and the big comfy bed. I guess that's what I needed." She stepped inside the kitchen and closed her eyes, inhaling deeply. "Twins."

"Yep. Twins."

Her stomach growled, loudly, and Margot smacked a hand to cover her face. "Oh. My. God."

"Hungry?" My lips twitched and her cheeks flamed.

"It would be silly to claim otherwise. Food would be great thanks. How can I help?"

I pointed to the cabinet above the coffee pot. "Plates are over there."

She nodded and moved around the kitchen easily, skirting around me as I stirred and added herbs and spices to the tomato sauce. It was like a well-choreographed dance, one we'd performed hundreds of times even though this was the first time. Margot set the table perfectly, because of course she did, lining up the silverware and even setting two glasses in front of each place setting. "Perfect."

I smiled and then frowned. "You keep linen napkins in your purse or something?"

She laughed prettily. "Nope, they're yours as it turns out."

I stared at the dark blue napkins folded into perfect triangles. "You're kidding."

"I'm not. They were in that drawer right there, along with a green and gold set."

I shrugged. "Must have been a gift from Mama or Beth." We settled at the table with more tea for Margot and a dark beer for me as we dug into the food. I gave her about five minutes of blissful eating before broaching her earlier shock. "Are you ready to talk about it now?"

She shook her head and started to blink fast. Too fast. "No," she said on a sob. "I'm not ready to talk about it, and

I'm certainly not ready for it to happen. Twins, Grady! I am entirely too old for twins. One baby was going to be difficult enough, but two? How can I possibly handle two babies while I run my business?"

"First of all, it's not just you. We will *both* have two babies to take care of while *we* run *our* businesses."

"Of course," she nodded. "You will be involved, but I'm the one carrying the food around."

I laughed. "Funny, they have these breast pumps that you can use so I can feed our babies later. Technology is amazing, ain't it?"

She glared at me. "Okay fine, together, but how will we do all this Grady? It was going to be difficult with one baby, but two?"

"We'll figure it out, the same way parents have been doing for thousands of years." I shrugged off her concern. "Besides, name one thing worth having that comes easy."

"Okay you might have a point there, but considering I'm hormonal with two babies growing inside of me, I reserve the right to freak out a little."

"A little?" I laughed and shook my head. "Freak out as much as you need. I'm right here. Me and my chicken riggies."

Margot ate her fill and pushed her plate away with a sigh. "Best riggies I ever had."

"That's what I like to hear. Go watch some TV while I clean up."

Margot shook her head. "I'm pregnant, not useless. I'll help."

I shrugged. "If you insist. I never turn down help when it comes to cleaning."

"Good to know."

We washed dishes together in companionable silence. I washed and she dried and put them away. It was all disturbingly domestic, except I wasn't disturbed by it at all. I wasn't uneasy, and I just fell into the movements with ease, like we'd been doing it forever.

And just like some type of modern day family, we finished in the kitchen and retired to bed like an old married couple.

It was the kind of domestic bliss I didn't think actually existed, and when Margot curled up against my chest, I allowed myself to enjoy the domesticity.

Just for tonight.

CHAPTER 19
MARGOT

I woke up in Grady's arms and it felt much better than I remembered. Waking up in Michael's arms certainly didn't stir me the way being pressed up against Grady's hard muscles and hot flesh did. It felt good. No, it felt better than good. It felt like heaven and bliss and want. My body pulsed with need—instead of nausea—first thing in the morning.

I smiled at that particular thought and turned to face him. In sleep, Grady was even more beautiful than when he was awake. Fiery gold lashes fanned against high cheekbones, his full lips parted into a slight smile as he slept, and this close without the intensity of his gaze staring back at me, I could see some of the freckles that were usually obscured because of his thick beard. Yeah, he was more than just good looking. More than handsome. He was truly beautiful in a really masculine way.

Feeling the devil on my shoulder I lifted one leg and rested on top of his hip, tracing his full lips with my fingertip. Grady stirred a little, a move that brought me within a breath of his morning erection. My nerves started to get the better of me and I moved to pull back, but Grady's hand shot out and gripped my hip. "Going somewhere?"

"Um," was the only word I could manage.

He smiled and popped open one blue eye and then the other. "You looking for trouble Margot?"

I smiled at the thick, rasp of his voice. "Is that what you named him, Trouble?"

A loud laugh erupted from Grady, and with how close we were, the sound vibrated my entire body and amplified my desire. He pulled me closer and flexed his hips so the full length and hardness of his erection pressed between my legs. He growled and I moaned, electricity sparked between us, and when Grady leaned in I was ready for his kiss.

Mostly.

I pulled back and he frowned. "Morning breath."

"Fuck morning breath," he growled and speared both hands through my hair and pulled me closer until our lips collided in a quick burst of lust that consumed us both. Lips and teeth and tongues bumped together in a clumsy dance born of early morning sleepiness and lust. Pure, unadulterated lust, and I had no objections.

None whatsoever.

Grady deepened the kiss while his hands roamed all over me. He gripped my hair tight around his fingers and kissed me like a man starved before his hands slid down my back and cupped my backside until I was on top of him, the long, thickness of him nestled between my thighs and I gasped. "Grady," I moaned and let my hips do the talking while his hands explored the changes in my body. He cupped my breasts under the t-shirt before he lifted it over my head and tossed it aside. My head fell back when his lips wrapped around my nipple and I cried out.

Grady paused. "Sensitive?"

I nodded. "But it feels good. Really good." To prove my point I arched into his touch, into his mouth and gripped his head in my hands to hold him right where I needed him.

Grady moaned, a deep and guttural sound that rocketed through my chest as he moved back and forth, tonguing my nipples and sucking hard. Sweat trickled down my back as my desire grew and my hips moved faster and faster. I was close, too close considering he was still wearing short boxer briefs. He pulled back with an exaggerated pop that made my nipples tingle. "Your breasts are a fucking work of art."

I shook my head and Grady flicked his tongue across my nipple. "They're just breasts."

He gripped my breasts in both hands and smashed them together so he could torture both of my nipples with his tongue while his hands massaged my plumpness until

I moaned. "These aren't *just* anything. These are magnificent, so don't argue with me about it."

I was tempted to argue, but then one hand slid down my waist and between my thighs where he found me hot and wet. "Oh!"

"So fucking wet," he growled and plunged one long finger deep.

"Yes Grady!" He fixed his mouth on my breasts while he squirmed out of his boxers and in the next moment his cock was long and thick, practically pulsing as he lowered me onto him. "Oh my...fuck."

"I love it when you talk dirty to me," he grinned and let his hands settle on my hips, giving me the power in that moment.

"You do?"

He nodded and licked his lips. "I love it more when your pussy squeezes my cock like this." He thrust his hips up and my head fell forward.

"Your cock is so hard," I told him, a little bit shy because dirty talk wasn't something I did, but his reactions had me reassessing my opinion. "So thick."

His grip tightened on my hips as they began to move faster and faster. "Margot," he roared and his hands moved from my hips to my breasts, squeezing them tight, his mouth lavishing love on my nipples while I took him deeper and harder. "Fuck yes."

He was so turned on that it turned me on even more,

and I gripped his shoulders and bounced harder and faster. "Grady, yes! More."

He growled and in a flash our positions were switched. His big body towered over me and his hips thrust faster and deeper, hitting me in that perfect spot until electric rainbows flashed behind my eyes. "Look at me," he moaned and licked a trail of heat across one breast and then the other.

"I see you," I panted and dug my heels into his lower back, urging him deeper still.

One hand slid between our bodies and he began to rub fast, intoxicating circles as his hips pumped a rapid beat. Deeper. Faster. He was a man on a mission with his jaws clenched and his blue gaze locked on my face. "I feel you coming," he smiled and rubbed faster circles against my clit. "So tight and wet on my cock."

His words were the magic that sent me over the edge for the longest orgasm of my entire life. My body shook and vibrated in waves as pleasure seeped out of me and I couldn't stop moving. My body was in control, and Grady kept pumping more pleasure into me, over and over. "You're getting even thicker," I grunted as another wave of pleasure knocked me backwards. "Oh!"

He took my mouth and kissed me deeply as if I mattered to him. Like I was a precious gift. Like I was his woman, all while his hips and fingers gave me more and more pleasure. And then his orgasm erupted in a loud roar against my mouth, his body jerked deeper into mine and another wave of orgasm took me under.

"Ah fuck, babe," he growled with satisfaction as my final orgasm came wetter and stickier than before. His hips moved and he grunted. "Oh fuck. I like that. A lot." Grady's lips brushed soft, gentle kissed on my cheek and my neck.

The doorbell chimed downstairs and we both froze. "Expecting company?" Instantly there was an image of a hungry lover showing up for sex.

"Nope," he smiled and kissed his way down my body until he was on his feet, scanning the room for something to wear. "I'll go get rid of them. You stay here."

His tone sent shivers of desire through me. "But-,"

Grady leaned over the bed and slid two fingers inside of me, triggering another much smaller orgasm. He flashed a satisfied smile. "Right. Here."

I nodded and collapsed against the bed with a well-loved smile on my face. I listened to Grady's bare feet on the steps, still smiling as I realized that while the sex was amazing, it was also Grady. I liked him more than I thought I would, and that's because he was nothing like the man I'd judged so harshly when he first came to town. He wasn't the playboy bartender I'd thought, instead he was so much more, and the more I knew about him, the more I wanted to know.

Voices drifted up from downstairs, low and serious,

which triggered all of my worst-case scenario fears and I jackknifed up in the bed. Something must be wrong for someone to show up unannounced so early in the morning. I found the t-shirt I'd slept in hanging off a chair beside the nightstand and slipped it over my head. It was not exactly appropriate for meeting a guest, but if you show up at the crack of dawn then you should expect people to be in a state of undress.

That's what I told myself as I crept down the stairs and found Grady deep in conversation with a short, plump woman with a mass of red and white curls.

She must have heard me, because she turned with a wide, knowing grin that was so similar to Grady's that I knew instantly they were related.

"I guess you two like each other well enough after all." She laughed good naturedly, and that put a smile on my face even if it was at my expense.

Grady looked mildly embarrassed but also amused. "Margot this is my Mama, Claire. Mama this is Margot."

"You don't say?" Her question was pure sarcasm, and I could see where Grady got his sense of humor.

"Behave Mama." He bussed her cheek and turned to me. "Your clothes are in the dryer, I'll see if they're ready and bring them up to you."

I nodded primly, falling back on my manners because I felt unsure of myself and embarrassed to be caught naked just moments after sex by his mother.

"I would appreciate that. A lot." Meeting the grandmother of my children for the first time in nothing but her son's t-shirt wasn't exactly the first impression I wanted to make.

CHAPTER 20
GRADY

"I didn't even get you a ticket yet." I made coffee to keep myself busy while I figured out the motive behind Mama's ambush visit. "Why didn't you call?"

Mama laughed and smacked the kitchen table. "This way was so much more fun," she answered. "Your Margot is pretty," she said, fishing.

"She's not mine." Not yet, but the way things were going between us, I could feel us getting closer, becoming more than sex buddies and future co-parents.

"She stayed the night, and that's not exactly your style."

"No," I admitted because a man couldn't lie to his mama. "We had the fifteen week checkup yesterday and found out some news that kind of shocked her. I brought her back here, ran her a bath and made dinner." How that small act of kindness had led to the smoke show this morning, I had no fucking clue, but I would keep it up for more of that.

"You are such a good boy Grady. She's lucky to have you."

"I am." Margot's voice sounded in the doorway of the kitchen and I wondered how much she'd heard. "Even if I'm only just starting to realize how lucky I am." She extended a hand to Mama and flashed a kind, yet nervous smile. "It's nice to meet you Claire. I am Margot Blanchard-Devereaux, and I've heard a lot about you."

Mama sized her up and then relaxed with a smile of her own. "I've heard a few things about you too, and I'm glad to see you and Grady have worked out your differences."

She looked to me in confusion at Mama's words, and I shrugged. "She's my mama. We talk."

Margot smiled softly at me, as if she was impressed by that admission.

"So Margot," Mama said and pat the seat beside her for Margot to sit. "What did the doctor say to spook you yesterday?"

She looked at me again with wide eyes and I shrugged. "We talk," I said again.

Resigned to the fact that there were no secrets between me and my Mama, Margot took the seat and nodded. "They told me that in here," she pointed at her belly. "Is two babies when I was expecting just one baby."

It took a moment for Mama to catch up, but when she gasped and smacked both hands over her mouth, I knew what was coming next. An excited whoop. "Twins! That is wonderful y'all, just wonderful!"

Margot is surprised. "You don't think I'm too old?"

Mama waved a dismissive hand at the question. "That's for the Lord to decide, and he gave you two babies instead of one, so clearly he thinks you're up to the task, and that's what matters." Mama gave her a sympathetic pat. "You have two babies to worry about Margot, so unless you're prancing around town in denim mini-skirts and tube tops, stop worrying about your age because it ain't gonna change. No matter how hard you try, and we *all* try."

"Thank you for that Claire. I can see where Grady's gets his gift for giving advice."

Mama threw her head back and laughed. "Buttering me up already. I like her Grady."

That was good to hear, because I was starting to like Margot too. A lot more than I thought was possible.

"Now that introductions are done, how about we go get some breakfast?"

Margot froze and I knew we were still a long way away from being okay.

CHAPTER 21
MARGOT

"I guess we know the father's identity *now*." A snide female voice came from behind me on the street, but I kept moving forward, refusing to let her words get to me.

Another snicker reached my ears. "I certainly wouldn't be keeping that hunk of man a secret."

"Right? Like she's *so* much better than him. Probably catfished him or something."

The women howled with laughter, and unlike typical Carson Creek gossip, this was mean spirited and borderline cruel. I walked a little faster to get out of earshot of the vultures I suspected were talking loud enough for me to hear on purpose.

"You two ought to be ashamed of yourselves, gossiping like this just because you can't land a man of your own. Maybe if you worked on being as pretty on the inside as you are on the outside you could catch a man like Grady." Claire gave the women a dismissive snort and called out to me.

"Wait up, girl. These legs aren't as young as they used to be."

I stopped and turned to Grady's mom with a smile. "Claire, this is a nice surprise."

"Would've been if not for those clowns." She shook her head and sent another glare at the women who had slowed down considerably, probably to avoid another run-in with my self-appointed bodyguard. "Get on out of here before I tell you what I really think."

At Claire's words they turned abruptly and did everything but ran away in their four-inch heels.

She laughed and looped her arm through mine. "Come on. I came into town hoping to buy you lunch."

"Oh you don't have to do that," I told her, half afraid of what she might say to me in Grady's absence.

"I know I don't have to, but I want to get to know you, and I've already made a reservation at Dark Horse. Grady says it's owned by some big shot music man."

I nodded. "Yes, and his wife runs the place. They have excellent food." I was about to suggest that she and Grady go there together, but Claire was a force of nature.

"Perfect. You can drive and I'll pay. Where did you park?"

Knowing there was nothing I could do to stop Hurricane Claire, I pointed in the direction where my car was parked, and with a resigned sigh made my way over. "This is me."

"Classic and classy," Claire hummed. "Exactly you."

I flashed a half-smile. "Thanks. I think."

We drove in silence for a couple of minutes, which is about how long it took to get to the Dark Horse at this time of day. As soon as the car was parked, Claire spoke.

"You've been avoiding Grady. Or me. Maybe both of us?"

She was one of the most direct women I had ever encountered, yet I was still surprised by her question. "Perhaps," I replied vaguely. I wanted to wait until we were seated with at least a modicum of privacy for this conversation. I had been avoiding Grady, but only because of the gossip. He'd never strayed too far from my mind even though I couldn't see him, which was as frustrating sexually as it was annoying.

Devon greeted us with a wide smile. "Good afternoon ladies. Table for two?"

"Yep, I made a reservation," Claire announced. "Claire McGraw."

Devon smiled and looked to the list for her name. "Got you right here, Mrs. McGraw. Is this your first time?"

"Sure is. I'm visiting my boy Grady, and figured this was a good time to get to know his baby mama." A soft squeak burst from my lips, and Claire gasped before she turned to me. "I assumed this whole town knew the way those women were talking. Sorry honey."

Devon grinned. "I already know," he assured Claire. "Right this way."

I followed Devon and Claire on wobbly legs, feeling as if I was having an out of body experience. I'd gone out of my way, most of my life, to make sure I was never the target of this type of gossip, and now it was all for nothing. Now my name was on the lips of every person in town under the age of ninety-nine.

"Your waitress will be with you shortly."

"Thank you, young man. You're not the music man, are you?"

Devon grinned. "No ma'am, but I've been his assistant for years and now I help run this place. He and Pippa are doing a photo shoot with Ryanna."

"Sounds glamorous," she sighed wistfully.

"Enjoy your meal," Devon said politely and turned on his heels to greet the next set of customers.

"All right Margot, *perhaps* you've been avoiding me and my son?"

I nodded. "I have a bit of an aversion to being the center of gossip, some might say it's a pathological aversion." Which again, was putting it mildly. "I know it's not Grady's fault, but avoiding him means avoiding more gossip."

Claire nodded. "Okay, but do you think that's fair to him?"

"No," I answered quickly. "I know it's not, but sometimes I just go into self-protection mode." I sighed heavily, reluctant to get into my own messed up childhood, but knowing it was the only way to explain. "I grew up with older parents, much older than my friends' parents, and they were never satisfied with anything I did. If I got an A, it should have been an A plus, so I worked harder and harder, but nothing was up to scratch."

"So you do the hoity-toity thing to keep people from getting too close?"

My shoulders sagged in relief. "In a nutshell, yes."

"I get that, believe me girly I understand that. But the thing is, when you make the choice to have kids, to share those children with another person, you have to find a way to change that. For the sake of the babies, because they will see how you act and they will do as Mommy does."

I let out a long breath at Claire's words and nodded. I hadn't thought of it like that. "I will endeavor to do better."

Claire laughed. "See, you're feeling defensive, and you get all high and mighty. Just ask yourself before you respond, does this person mean me harm? I only want the best for you, my boy and those babies. That's it."

The waitress came and took our order, giving me a necessary break from the emotional conversation. "I believe you, but Grady is your son, so you want what's best for him."

"And believe it or not Margot, I think that's you."

I blinked in disbelief. "I don't, no, I *can't* believe that.

I'm too old for him, and this pregnancy wasn't planned. We weren't even in a relationship and now we're tethered together for life."

"Doesn't matter how you get there, as long as you do," she said easily and sipped her whiskey lemonade. "Grady is a good man, and with the right woman he's gonna be a great man. But a woman like you probably expects flowers and chocolate and jewelry to know a man cares, and that's just not Grady, not before the money, and not after. His love language is service Margot. He does for you because he cares for you."

I shook my head. "He does for me because I'm carrying his children."

"And running that bath was just for the babies? The sex after you found out you were pregnant? The meals? Meeting me?" Claire shook her head in displeasure. "He cares about you, and it's as clear as day. If you would open your eyes without the lenses of your past, you would see that."

"I've been looking at everything through those lenses Claire, I don't know how to view the world any other way."

"Straightforward," she said, as if it were just that simple. "That blouse makes your boobies look fantastic. That's honest and straightforward."

I laughed. "Thanks?"

"You're welcome. Has Grady lied to you? Given you a reason he might say something just to spare your feelings?

Because I'm his Mama and he rarely does it for me, and almost never for Beth. It's not his style."

I felt like she was trying to tell me something but it was getting muddled, or maybe I was just incapable of understanding.

"No, as far as I can tell he has been nothing but honest with me, even when I didn't want him to be."

Claire huffed out a laugh. "That's my boy. He won't spare your feelings, but he will always make sure you *feel* cared for and loved. He bought me a house in a place he knew I would enjoy living, so I would always have a place to call home, and even though I miss him like crazy since he moved out here, that's the kind of act of love that forgives a lot."

The waitress brought our food to the table and we ate in silence for a few minutes, both of us taking in what's been said. But I felt as if Claire was trying to tell me something, to guide me, and I wanted to know what she was getting at. Explicitly.

"What are you saying Claire?"

"I'm saying that rich girls like you always expect big proclamations, grand gestures you call them, but the fact is that's not my boy. Oh sure he'll tell you he loves you when the time is right, but men can—and do—say a lot of things they don't mean. Grady will show you in more ways than you know exist, how he feels about you. You just have to keep those pretty little eyes open, or you'll miss the signs."

miss the signs. I thought about all the thoughts of Grady over the past few days that refused to leave my mind. He was a man who took care of those he cared about, like the way he let Carlotta take over his bar for events, even though it was clear he didn't like it and didn't need the money. He'd taken care of me despite the awful things I'd said to him over the past year, and he'd stepped up to donate to the July Fourth block parties. He was a good man, a good neighbor and I was...not.

"You're right Claire. You are absolutely right, and if I don't do something about it, I'm just going to end up another regret." Like Michael and all the others.

Claire flashed a satisfied smile. "Just what I wanted to hear." She lifted another piece of steak and chewed slowly. "That's good steak. While I'm here I want to help you start setting up for the babies. A nursery for starters, not to mention a stroller, car seats and basinets. Double everything."

"Yes, sure," I said slightly distracted by more thoughts of Grady.

By the time our lunch was over, I was eager to get to Grady's Bar, to set eyes on him after nearly a week apart. I was starved for a glimpse of him, and I was in an aroused state at the distinct lack of Grady the past few mornings. And evenings.

"Are you going back to Grady's?"

"Nah," Claire sighed. "He's busy working, and that big ol' house has nothing for me to do but cook. I saw a yarn store in town that I want to check out since I need to make hats and booties for twins."

Perfect. The Yarn Store was just a block away from Grady's bar, which meant I could drop her off without letting on that I was putting her advice into action immediately.

"If you need a ride before Grady is done, just give me a call."

"Good to be the boss huh?"

I laughed. "Something like that, yeah. Happy shopping."

"Any color preferences for the babies?"

I thought about it for a second and shrugged. I hadn't given much thought to the gender of my babies yet, because everything else was so overwhelming.

"No. Go crazy."

Claire laughed. "You asked for it."

I felt good as I walked with determination into the bar. Claire was as kooky as they came, but she was wonderful. Loving and caring, and she was excited about her first grandchildren. More family to love my babies was a blessing I wouldn't take for granted. And Grady, well he was a different beast altogether.

The bar was busier than usual this time of day when I stepped inside, but I ignored the chaos and went in search of Grady, which didn't take long. He was on one side of the bar—his usual side—and a busty blond in skin tight shorts was draped across his chest even with the length of the bar between them. Grady's smile was tight as the woman laughed obnoxiously.

"Oh come on bartender, just one little smooch."

His hands went to her waist and I didn't wait to see where they roamed on her curves, or where his mouth landed on her plump red lips. I rushed from the bar, willing the tears that burned the backs of my eyes to go away. Far, far away. That was the kind of woman Grady should be with. She was young-ish, fit and fun, not fat and pregnant and always sick. I felt like a fool for letting myself hope that a man like Grady would want a woman like me.

I'd let the words of a loving mother confuse my mind as well as my heart.

Grady wasn't into me in a romantic sense, he was here out of a sense of obligation and responsibility. It wasn't affection, and it definitely wasn't love. "Love, hardly," I grunted as tears blurred my vision and I stumbled down the street. "Love doesn't humiliate." He had to know that word of his antics would get back to me since the whole town now knew he was the father of my children.

He knows but he doesn't care.

And why should he? Grady didn't owe me anything, and with my vanishing act over the past week he was free to do what he wanted. *And he did,* that snide voice in my head said to me.

Whatever. It didn't matter. As long as he stepped up where the kids were concerned then I would be happy.

Single parenthood wouldn't be so bad. I had friends, a support system of sorts, and I had money to hire help when I needed it. No big deal.

No problem at all.

I swiped at the tears and nearly stumbled to the ground at the curb. Where I was going, I hadn't a clue, but I needed to walk off this anger and humiliation. I needed to get as far away from Grady as possible, so I continued on a forward trajectory. Carson Creek was small enough that I could just walk back to my car when I was in the mental headspace to operate a vehicle. I walked in a straight path with no regard to anyone or anything but my hurt feelings. I ignored my name being called, greetings and even a loud honk of a horn that was close.

Too close.

I froze and swiped my eyes just in time to see a big green Cadillac barreling towards me. I jumped back with enough room to spare to avoid getting hit by a car, but my hip smacked against the truck parked at the corner and I fell backwards on the oddly warm concrete. Shouts sounded and then hurried footsteps, Claire's worried face was the last thing I saw before everything faded to black.

CHAPTER 22
GRADY

The bar doors smacked open and Carlotta appeared first followed by Mama. Instantly my heart skidded to a halt.

"What?" They both wore worried expressions, as if someone had died and there was only one person I could think of, hell one person I hadn't stopped thinking of even though she'd gone and pulled another vanishing act for the past week. "I said what?"

Carlotta's hands fidgeted in the fabric of her dress and Mama was a ghostly shade of white. "It's Margot," Carlotta finally spat out.

"She hit her head and they took her to the hospital," Mama filled in the rest. "I'll stay here," she urged. "You should go be with her."

I nodded and absently looked around the bar as if there was anything more important in the world at the moment than Margot's well-being. Too many emotions warred within me, and I didn't have time to settle on just one. "I'm going. Thanks for letting me know." I kissed Mama's cheek and squeezed Carlotta's shoulder before I made my way outside and jumped in my car.

The fucking hospital. She'd worked herself up into such a tizzy she ended up in the ER, and by the time a nurse showed me to her room, I was good and worried and twice as pissed off.

"Grady? What are you doing here?"

I whirled on her with a wicked expression on my face. "Well I was deep inside the blond that sent you running, but I figured you being the mother of my kids and all, I should make sure you were all doing all right." My tone was harsh, I knew that. Despite the relief I felt that she was fine, I couldn't stop the flood of angry words. "What in the hell were you thinking Margot? Oh, besides the fact that I'm some piece of shit who would publicly humiliate you."

"Grady, please."

I shook my head. "I saw you come in, you know. I saw you, and I waited for you to come to the bar, but you never did."

"You were busy," she said with a pout, her gaze fixed out the window because she refused to look at me. "With that woman."

I stared at her in disbelief, though I really wasn't surprised in the least. It was always going to end up here.

Fucking always. "So you were jealous because some woman was flirting with me, the lowly bartender you barely even like? Or was it that she was young and hot, and not pregnant?"

"Don't be a jerk."

"Only you're allowed to be a jerk?" I asked. "Classic Margot. You know, I really thought things had changed between us, that you'd started to see me, the real me instead of the guy you conjured up in your head."

She folded her arms. "I saw what I saw, Grady."

"And what exactly did you see besides some drunk wannabe country star with her paws all over me? She was drunk and threatening to go out to Derek's place to record with him. I called him and he asked me to keep her there so she didn't hurt herself, or end up getting hurt by Bella." I shook my head again. "I didn't kiss her, didn't encourage her flirting, and I didn't go home and fuck her, so I don't really see what I did that was so horrible." I paced the length of the hospital room and fumed. After everything I'd done the past few months to show her I was a standup guy, none of it mattered. "You never planned on seeing me differently," I accused.

"I am old and fat and pregnant, Grady. Excuse me for being jealous of some woman hanging on you who is my exact opposite."

I huffed out a laugh. "What do you even care, Margot? You clearly don't like me or trust me, so what difference does it make who flirts with me? I'm a bartender, that's what people do. They flirt and tell me their problems."

"Of course I care," she roared and then gripped her head as she cried out in pain.

"Relax," I told her in a much calmer voice than I felt. "You're only those things in your head, fat and pregnant and old. None of that is what I think about you, it's all in your head." I sighed and dropped down in the hard plastic chair with a grunt. "I'm here because I want to be, because despite my best efforts, I like you. A lot. And you're in this bed all because of how poorly you think of me."

"It's not you Grady."

"Of course it's me!" I jumped from the chair and started to pace the room once again. "I should have listened to you from the start. You think I'm trash, and you're only allowing me to be involved because you have no choice." As the truth really and truly dawned on me, I felt like an idiot. "You told me time and again what you thought of me and I refused to listen."

"I was wrong," she insisted through tears. "That's what I was coming to tell you."

"Yeah? You must have really meant it to have your opinion change so quickly. You must have really believed it to run into oncoming traffic."

"Grady," she cried out. "Stop. Please." She covered her eyes in shame or pain, it was hard to tell at the moment, and that made me feel bad.

The hospital door burst open and Mama stepped

inside looking mad enough to spit fire. "I heard the yelling down the hall. What the hell is going on in here?"

"Nothing. Apparently."

Mama's eyes missed nothing, not Margot's tears and not the way my nostrils flared angrily. "All right. Emotions are high right now, so Grady go take a walk while I sit with Margot for a while."

I wanted to argue, but I also wanted to be gone, so I nodded and stepped outside the room and continued to pace the floor until the tiles started to wear thin.

Margot was who she was, and as a man who often marched to my own beat I understood and respected that. Which meant it was time to stop waiting for Margot to see what she was intentionally blind to, and it was time to accept her for the woman she was, because that wasn't going to change.

I would take care of her in any way that I could, that she would allow.

Otherwise I would do exactly as she had done. I would keep my distance.

CHAPTER 23
MARGOT

Claire paced the length of my room the same way her son had, the only difference being that she didn't radiate quite as much righteous anger as Grady had. She was angry without a doubt, but it was more subdued, almost understanding.

"Don't hold it in Claire, it's not good for a woman your age." She looked at me with fury in her eyes and I shrugged. In for a penny, in for a pound I figured.

"I just want to throttle you Margot, and I don't mean just shake some damn sense into you, I mean I want to take these fists and pound them into you until you can see things clearly." She stopped pacing and let out a heavy sigh full of exasperation and exhaustion. "Margot, sweetheart you shaved about a decade off my life. You know that right?"

I could see how worried she was about me, and that

filled me with guilt. This woman who didn't know me a month ago was so worried about me that it made her angry, the thought of serious injury or worse.

"I know, and I'm sorry, but it's not like I did it on purpose."

She nodded as if she understood, but she didn't. She couldn't. Claire was a force of nature in her own right, so she had no idea how it felt to constantly doubt and wonder. "Maybe you didn't mean to walk out into traffic and crack your noggin on the concrete, but your insecurity made sure that was inevitable. Margot," she sighed. "Grady is handsome and well-built and successful in his own right, I know that as well as you. He could have had any woman he wanted, and he chose you."

I swallowed around the lump in my throat caused by that particular truth. "So you *do* get it."

She nodded. "The same way that you're beautiful and successful and could have gotten knocked up by any man you wanted, but you chose my boy on that particular night. Why?"

My mouth opened and shut like a fish struggling to breathe outside water.

Claire pointed at me, fire in her eyes. "Because despite the way you both lie to yourselves about the animosity between you, there's something there. Something more than physical attraction and mutual dislike. There's something real there, but you two dummies are two damned scared to admit it to yourselves or to each other." Claire shook her head, disgusted. "Do you want to do this on your own Margot? Is that your goal?"

"No," I admitted to her as well as to myself. "I'm not sure that I can even if I wanted to." Raising twins alone while running a business was not something I could do on my own, I could admit that much, but I didn't know how to change or how to make it right.

"Are you sure? Because you're doin' everything in your power to push Grady away. Men are more fragile than we are Margot, if they feel they aren't wanted or needed then they will just pick up stakes, move on and never look back. It's their superpower."

My heart seized at the idea of Grady picking up stakes —literally or figuratively—and moving away, forgetting all about me and our babies.

"I'm not trying to."

"I know," she said softly, her tone and demeanor gentle and understanding. She moved to the bed and leaned over to wrap me in her arms before she pressed a kiss to my cheek. "You're allowed to be emotional because you're hormonal and pregnant, and that's just the way things are, but you are not allowed to try to kill my grandbabies. Not ever. Do that again and I'll be bunking with you until they finish high school."

How I managed to laugh in that moment when my head ached and it felt as if everyone close to me hated me or was angry with me—or both—I will never know. But thanks to Claire my shoulders shook with laughter and I nodded my understanding.

"I'll keep that in mind."

Claire pulled back with a satisfied smile and patted my cheek. "That's what I want to hear, honey. Grady is upset now because he's scared, but he'll get over it. If you do your part to make this work. Whatever it is."

I nodded at Claire's words, because I had no idea what Grady and I were besides future co-parents and former sex partners, but also kind of current sex partners. There were no defined lines between us, and that made everything even more confusing.

"I'm working on it." It wasn't something I could change with the snap of my fingers, but as I watched Claire exit my hospital room, my head throbbing, I really wished that magical switch did exist.

Grady and I were fooling ourselves. There's no way to turn a one night stand into something more, something substantive. He will make a great father, but does that make him the man for me? Unlikely. My head hurt just thinking about it, but I knew I had to think about it, had to figure it out before the babies arrived, if for no other reason than to make our lives easier.

Fifteen minutes later Grady walked into the room with a stormy expression on his face, but he didn't give me more grief, instead he was eerily silent.

Thankfully the doctor arrived shortly after Grady, which gave me something else to focus on instead of the giant blue-eyed, tattooed man who could barely look at me. The doctor's gaze slid to Grady and then back to me.

"Margot, how are we feeling?"

"Besides the giant headache? Not too bad."

"That's good to hear, considering everything that's happened." He looked down at the chart in his hands and sighed. "But you have a sprained wrist and a concussion, which means you need to be watched closely for the next twenty-four hours." He looked to Grady again. "Do you have someone to do that for you?"

"She does," Grady answered before I could. "What am I watching for?"

"Bleeding, incoherence, nausea or double vision, balance issues and confusion. She will need to be watched closely and checked on often."

Grady gave one stiff nod. "That won't be a problem."

It won't? He could barely look at me, but he was taking responsibility for my physical well-being for the next twenty-four hours? It didn't make any sense.

"Grady that's not necessary," I started, but he cut me off.

"It's done," he practically growled in my direction even as he still only glanced in my general direction, his eyes never actually met mine. "When will Margot be discharged?"

The doctor looked concerned, but he hid it well with a nod and a professional smile. "It will take a few hours, but no more than three or four until she's fully discharged with instructions for care."

Grady nodded and stood in the corner beside the window with his arms folded, a blank expression on his face that bordered on angry. As soon as the doctor exited the room, Grady was practically on his heels.

"I'll be back soon."

He didn't look back, didn't ask me how I was feeling or even spare one glance for me, and I was pretty sure that I've ruined things between us completely.

There was nothing to be done at the moment, so I waited for *something*, for anything to happen. For the next four hours I sat in bed and waited. And waited.

CHAPTER 24
GRADY

Damn stubborn woman.

I should have known she would find a reason to screw up the modicum of peace we had going between us. We were doing fine, more than fine. Hell, better than fine. Between the sex and the way she was letting me be there for her, I should have known that it was all temporary. Margot was who she was, and though she would kill me for saying so, she was apparently too old to change.

So why in the hell was I inside her house and packing bags of clothing and toiletries and other creature comforts to make her happy while she was on concussion watch? Because I was clearly a glutton for punishment. But she was the mother of my children and she needed someone to look after her, to make sure she was all right, which would mean that my babies were all right, so I took the bags to my house and set her up in the second guest room. I made sure her clothes were hung up, the toiletries were set up in the bathroom, and I put the small fridge in the garage in her room and filled it with sparkling water and ginger ale. Margot would have everything she needed to stay at my place until she was feeling better.

When I was satisfied the guest room was good enough, I returned to the hospital, tired and angry and in no mood to stick to social niceties. The nurses smiled as they gave me verbal and written instructions on how to care for Margot for the next twenty-four hours and I tried to smile back, but it felt more like a grimace.

Mama was in Margot's room and they were laughing and smiling when I went inside, my presence stopped them cold. "Ready to go?"

Margot nodded and looked around the room. "Um, yes. I think so."

I held up a bag and dropped it at the foot of her bed. "I brought you a change of clothes."

"Thanks," she said, surprised that an asshole like me would do anything kind for her.

"Yep." I waited in the hall until Mama's hand squeezed my shoulder.

"Take it easy on her Grady. She's emotional and confused, and she needs you more than you realize."

"She doesn't need me for a damn thing Mama, and that's fine. Those babies will need me and that's my focus." And as soon as they arrived safely in this world,

Margot and I could maintain an even greater, even cooler distance.

"You're wrong," she sighed. "I just hope you two figure it out before there's too much between you to bridge the gap." She shook her head and went back inside Margot's hospital room and I stayed where I was.

Inside the car Mama chatted up Margot the whole ride home, laughing it up as if she hadn't nearly died and taken my babies with her. I could feel the weight of Margot's gaze on me, curious and almost pleading for me to glance at her, to give her another minute of my attention.

I refused to give in. All I had to offer was what she needed at the moment, someone to watch her overnight.

Nothing more.

"Where are we going?" Margot asked in an almost stammering voice.

"To my place. For now." I pulled into the driveway and helped Margot inside and up the stairs to the guest room. I was a good man and I didn't need to keep trying to prove it to her, so I was done trying. Margot would never believe it and that was on her, not me.

"This isn't necessary Grady." Her tone was wary, as if she expected me to put her in my room. In my bed.

I bypassed my room and took her to the guest room I set up for her. "Everything you need should be here, if it's not, you know where to find me." Not that I was holding my breath. Margot would rather die than admit she needed me for anything.

"Grady this is...too much." She shook her head as she looked around the room in awe. "I don't know what to say."

"Don't say anything," I told her because there was nothing to say, and I didn't want her damned gratitude.

"Listen Grady, I owe you an apology. Probably several if we're being honest-,."

I shook my head. "Just relax Margot. Take it easy and dinner will be ready soon." I left her room without another word and marched down the hall to my room for a quick shower before I made my way downstairs where Mama had already started on dinner. "You don't need to do that."

Mama turned to me with a sly smile. "I don't need to, but I figured you could use the help."

"Thanks," I grunted and gathered more ingredients to season the beef.

Mama sighed and leaned against the counter beside me. "Take it easy on her, son."

"I am," I insisted. "I'm giving her exactly what she wants by helping make her life easier without imposing my low class presence on her." I thought things were changing between us, but they weren't. "Things aren't going to change, and I'm learning to accept that Mama. You should too."

She let out a snorting laugh and shook her head. "Bullshit. You're scared of what you feel for her and you're running scared."

"Of course I care," I growled. "But that hasn't gotten

me anywhere good. She nearly killed herself because she thinks I'm such a piece of shit that I would humiliate her in front of the whole damn town, so yeah I'm done. She got her wish. I will take care of her and my babies, but with a healthy distance between us."

Mama stared at me for a long time as if she was looking at a stranger. Her eyes studied me carefully and she sighed again. "You could try talking to her instead of falling into bed every chance you get."

I shook my head. "It won't work. I've tried to talk to her, but she doesn't want me to know her, not the real her anyway. I've gotten glimpses of her, but I'm not the man she wants so I'm not privy to that part of her. I'm not the man she pictured for her happy ending and she refuses to see an alternate ending, so this is where we are Mama. Exactly nowhere."

With those words I turned my attention back to dinner and lost myself in the details of caramelizing carrots, smashing potatoes and chopping herbs. Worrying about food was better and more productive than worrying about a woman who would rather cut off her nose just to spite her face instead of admitting there was something between us.

Because there isn't.

There was nothing between us other than a few really hot nights and a lifetime of parenting our twins together.

Eventually that would be enough for me.

CHAPTER 25
MARGOT

Things were so tense at Grady's house that I felt as if I was constantly walking on eggshells. Not that it was necessary, of course, because other than taking care of my basic needs, Grady behaved as if I didn't exist. If not for Claire I would spend most days in complete and total silence. The last words Grady had uttered to me centered around questions about the current president, what year it was, and my current location, this was to ensure my concussion hadn't gotten any worse.

It hadn't.

And things between Grady and I hadn't improved either, and it was all my fault. My own silly insecurities put me in this position, and I had no choice but to deal with it. Like a grownup.

Which I was.

Mostly.

I jumped at the sound of a rapid knock on the door and quickly got to me feet. Even it was just a delivery driver, some interaction was better than none since Claire had gone to get more yarn with a promise to return with something delicious for lunch. I opened the door so quickly I almost fell backwards but caught myself in time as my brows dipped into a confused frown.

"What are you ladies doing here?" Pippa, Lacey, Carlotta and Valona all stood in the doorstep with uncertain smiles and bags.

"We're here to make sure you're all right."

My frown deepened. "All right? Why wouldn't I be all right?" My lips trembled at the kind gesture from women I'd known all of my life but had never really made an effort to truly befriend except Carlotta, and that was only because our businesses forced us together often.

Carlotta stepped forward first. "Because honey, you're a mess, and you're pregnant, and we've come with reinforcements."

I stepped back and motioned for them to enter. "What kind of reinforcements? And what makes you think I'm a mess?"

"Mama Claire told us," Carlotta said as if she'd known the woman forever.

I should have known Claire hadn't gone through that

giant bag of yarn so quickly. "Claire asked you to come over." They hadn't come because they truly cared.

"No, Claire said you and Grady needed to be sorted out," Valona clarified. "So here we are."

"And we brought gifts," Pippa said. "Perfect for a pregnant woman about to blow her life to pieces, plus a few adorable things for the baby."

"Babies," Carlotta clarified.

"Twins?" Lacey echoed.

I nodded. "Yes, twins. I'm forty-seven and I'm pregnant with twins."

"Well damn," Pippa grunted. "Looks like we'll have to get two of everything."

I looked at the women who were all smiles, happy for what they saw as my good fortune, and I didn't know what to do other than cry. "You didn't have to do this," I sniffled. "I haven't been a good friend to any of you, and I don't deserve this."

Lacey laughed and wrapped an arm around me as she guided me into the kitchen with the others right behind us. "Margot you're a little uptight and distant, always have been, but that doesn't mean your friends won't show up when you need them. You need us, and here we are."

I cried even harder at her words and shook my head. "I ruined everything with Grady. Before I even knew what was happening or what I wanted, I ruined it."

"It can't be all that bad," Carlotta insisted and pushed my shoulders down until I was seated. "You're here in his house, which I assume means that he's taking care of you."

"He is," I admitted with a sigh. "He's great actually. He went to my house and got a bunch of clothes and toiletries for me, even my favorite pillow and some of my teas. He cooks meals all the time, and when he can't he sends food to make sure I'm eating. He made sure I had my laptop so I could work while I'm here."

The women all looked at each other in confusion, but Carlotta spoke for them. "Sound great. What's the problem then?"

"He put me in his guest room. We've been sleeping together regularly since we learned of the pregnancy, and now he put me in the guest room. That's a pretty clear sign that I ruined things."

"Ouch," Pippa agreed with a frown. "He's hurt."

"Definitely," Valona added with a nod. "If you want things back to the way they were, or whatever you want, you'll need to make it up to him."

"Unless you're just worried that this means he'll leave you to do it all on your own," Carlotta asked bluntly.

I shook my head. "He won't do that. Grady wants to be involved in the pregnancy and the babies. He will be there for them until he takes his last breath."

"So this is about him," Val guessed correctly. "You care about him more than you've let on, probably more than you're willing to admit to yourself." Valona shook her head and pursed her lips. "He's operating in the dark Margot which is unfair. You need to talk to him."

"I know," I admitted reluctantly and leaned back into the kitchen chair while Lacey and Pippa unpacked bags of food that included potato salad, a cheese and meat board, barbecue shredded pork and stuffed mushrooms. "I've tried. For two weeks I have tried to engage him in conversation, but he won't budge. He asks me how I am, how I'm feeling and what I want for dinner." It was embarrassing to admit. "When I try to apologize for my behavior, he tells me not to worry about it. Says *I heard you loud and clear Margot, and I'm giving you what you want, but I'm not leaving my babies.* What the hell is that?"

"You pushed him away," Lacey guessed. "He resisted until it became clear to him that what you really wanted was this, him to be around to help out and nothing more."

Valona nodded. "Operating in the dark until he figured out what you were doing. I tried that with Trey and he called me on it."

"Then maybe that's a sign that Grady doesn't want me that way."

Valona laughed. "Or it's a sign that he shows his love in different ways. Just a thought," she shrugged and reached for the bowl of potato salad.

Carlotta piled some of everything on a plate and set it in front of me before she took the seat closest to me. "His mama is here, and if I were you I'd pump her for information that would help me get back inside his heart. But only if you're ready to hand yours over as well and tell him those three words."

I shook my head immediately. "I can't do that. I promised myself after Michael that I wouldn't fall in love ever again. I just can't do that. I have a terrible track record that proves I am horrible at relationships." My heart raced at the idea of saying those words to Grady and being met with silence. "I'll find a way to make things right and friendly again. That's all I need." The lie felt like sawdust on my tongue.

Valona shook her head and laughed. "No offense Margot, but if I can open my heart to a man far too gorgeous for me after what Rodney did, then you can sure as hell admit to Grady that you love him."

I shook my head. "I can't. I've been so awful to him."

"And if you actually felt awful about it," Carlotta said with a friendly smile that took the sting off her tone, "then you would do something about it. Don't wait for him to listen, *make* him listen."

"You can't make a man like Grady do anything he doesn't want to do, and clearly talking to me is at the top of that list."

"Make it impossible for him to ignore you," Lacey offered. "Show up in his bed naked and refuse to go anywhere until he listens."

"And risk that rejection? No thanks."

Pippa sighed and pointed at my plate to encourage me to eat. "I'm sorry to say this Margot, but if you're too scared to risk rejection then you don't deserve the happiness that comes with being in love."

Carlotta nodded her agreement. "Grady is great. He's gruff sure, but he's sweet and funny, and he is always willing to help out however he can. You could do a lot worse than Grady, and considering your track record, I'm sorry to say that you have."

"Ouch."

Carlotta flashed a wide, friendly smile. "That's why I said I'm sorry to say it."

"You didn't sound sorry though," Lacey stage whispered and the rest of us laughed.

"Okay, let's say that I was brave enough to force him to listen and to risk rejection, is there anything I could actually do or say to earn his forgiveness?"

Pippa, Valona and Lacey all looked to Carlotta who knew Grady best.

Carlotta sighed. "Show him that he is enough for you. That you don't actually care that he works at the bar he owns, that you don't think he's some low class trash. And also tell him those same things and do it in no uncertain terms."

"Oh," I deadpanned. "Is that all?"

The women laughed. "It's scary as hell," Lacey admitted. "But worth it."

"Definitely worth it," Pippa said with a smile. "You think I wanted to trust Ryan again after everything? I didn't, but I also couldn't deny that no one had ever made me feel the way I feel when I'm with him."

"Dammit," I growled because that's how I felt about Grady. He wasn't who I would have chosen for myself, but he was who my heart had chosen because he accepted me as I was and let me be me, and seemed to love me anyway.

At least I hoped he did.

CHAPTER 26
GRADY

"Two pitchers of frozen strawberry margaritas, and one pitcher lemon-lime on the rocks. Rocks separately," I told the group of after work happy hour women with my best, most charming smile. "Cheers ladies."

The women were rowdy and filled with laughter. "Cheers right back 'atcha handsome."

I flashed a smile I didn't feel and ambled back to the bar to pour beers for a few of the regulars who kept their gazes fixed on the televisions above and steadfastly read world and sports news all night. I made more Happy Hour specials as more and more of the five o'clock crowd spilled inside and filled the place. Business was booming, but I couldn't enjoy any of it, because of Margot.

The past few weeks had been tense. Hell, they were more than tense. It was a silent battle of wills between me and the stubborn woman who carried my kids. She wanted to talk, but it was only because her fine southern sensibilities made her incapable of dealing with someone who was angry or didn't like her, which was her problem not mine. I wouldn't allow her to apologize simply to make herself feel better. She had to mean it or keep it to her damn self.

"Cheer up boy, this joint is jumpin'." Mama's voice pulled me from my thoughts and I flashed her a grateful smile.

"Hey Mama. What are you doing here?"

She shook her head. "You first. Why the hangdog expression?"

"Don't know what you're talking about."

She let out a loud bark of laughter which drew a few stares. "You can lie to the world, son. You can even lie to yourself, but you can never, ever lie to your mama. I know you, and I know you're upset. I even know why, but I thought it'd be polite to let you tell me yourself."

I laughed at her. "Thanks Mama, but I'm good. Just busy tonight."

She swiveled on her bar stool and nodded at the crowded bar. "As the owner this should please you."

"It does, but it also tires me out."

"Bullshit."

I blinked. "Mama," I chided. "Such language from a lady."

She laughed again. "Boy I ain't never claimed to be

anybody's lady." Her laughter faded and Mama shook her head again. "She's hurting too, you know."

I shook my head. "She just doesn't like it because she thinks I'm mad at her."

"Aren't you?"

I was, but not anymore. "Nope. I'm respecting her wishes. She did everything in her power to push me away and now that I've taken the hint, she's playing the part of the victim." It was exactly why I kept my relationships short, sweet and uncomplicated.

"Not everything is as straightforward as you want it to be Grady."

"Not everything, no. But this is." My stomach turned over as I thought of the idiot I'd been over yet another snooty rich girl. "It's fine Mama. We have time to learn how to parent the kids together, to be civil and maintain a platonic relationship. It will be fine."

"Fine yes, but is that what you really want? To watch the woman that you love and your kids end up happy with someone else while you stand on the sidelines and watch?"

"Doesn't matter what I want."

"You could listen to what she has to say. She might surprise you."

"Doubtful," I snorted and moved down the bar to make drinks for half a dozen new customers. I turned to grab cocktail glasses and ran into Mama. "What are you doing back here?"

"I'm helping out," she said as if it were just that simple. "Margot just called, and she needs you. Go to her and I'll take care of this place."

I shook my head. "She didn't call me, so I'm guessing she needs *you*. Go."

Mama shook her head and leaned over the bar towards the county prosecutors. "What'll be gents, gin or vodka martinis?"

"Gin," they replied in chorus, and Mama smiled.

"Good boys." She reached for the top shelf gin and a shaker before she nodded to be. "Go on. She's expecting you."

Mama's serious expression put me on edge, and even though I knew she was up to something, the part of me that worried about Margot and the babies got me moving towards the back office and then to the back exit where my car was parked. I paused a stop signs and pushed the speed limit as I rushed back to my place to check on Margot.

The house was dark as I pulled into the driveway and my heart sped up. Had she fallen in the dark? Was there a power outage in the area? I ran inside and called out for Margot, smacking the wall to check the lights, all of which came on as I rushed through the house.

"Margot!"

"Back here," she called out, no signs of distress in her voice, which slowed me down.

Mama was definitely up to something. "What's wrong?" I asked from the doorway of the kitchen.

Margot stood in the middle of the candlelit kitchen with a nervous expression on her face, a deep burgundy lingerie set showed off her beautiful pregnant boobs and her round belly. "Nothing," she said with a sigh. "Or maybe everything. I'm not quite sure."

At her words my shoulders relaxed. Nothing was wrong. Margot and the babies were safe. Me? Not so much. "I was working Margot, and I thought something was seriously wrong."

"Something is wrong Grady. Between us everything is wrong lately."

I sighed and dropped down into one of the kitchen chairs. "I've given you exactly what you wanted Margot, and you're still not happy. This is just your problem, and I can't do anything to fix that. More importantly, I won't."

She flashed a heartbreaking smile and nodded. "You're right. It was all about me Grady and it was never about you, my attitude I mean. You are…a lot. Big and gorgeous, and totally comfortable in your own skin. Even being looked at as an outsider in a small gossipy town didn't seem to shake you at all, but for someone like me, that's a terrifying prospect." Her nervous smile cracked the ice around my heart, damn her. "I knew if I was too nice to you, or if I let you get too close, even as a casual acquaintance, that I would fall under your spell. I couldn't risk it, not again. So I was terrible to you."

I couldn't deny that her words shocked me. "So let me get this straight, you were mean to me because you were afraid you might like me?"

A bubble of laughter exploded out of Margot. "Pretty much."

I stood and stared at her for a long time, wondering what the purpose of the lingerie was, but too afraid to ask, because I couldn't risk falling under her spell. Again.

"Thank you for telling me." I turned with the intention of heading back to my bar.

"Grady, wait! Please."

I stopped. "You've said what you have to say Margot, and now I'm leaving."

"No you're not," she growled and shuffled across the kitchen to block my path. "I've only just begun with what I need to say to you, and this isn't easy, so you damn well will listen to me!" Her chest heaved up and down, the pulse in her throat fluttered like butterfly wings and I could see how difficult this was for her.

I took a step back and nodded. "Fine. Talk."

CHAPTER 27
MARGOT

I sighed heavily, but I refused to let my shoulders sag or my hope fade in the face of Grady's reluctant tone. *Fine, talk* wasn't exactly the sign of a man willing to listen and to hear what's being said to him, but I had the captive audience I wanted and I had to make it work. He stood on one side of the kitchen and I stood at the other, a vast ocean between us that I was desperate to close.

Now.

I swallowed around the gigantic lump in my throat and nodded until I felt the confidence within me rise to the surface. This was Grady. He was a good man, a fair man who would hear me out without being mean or cruel. The only thing he could do was reject me, and it wouldn't be the first—or the last—so I could handle it.

Mostly.

Hopefully.

"I grew up with parents who were great. They had plenty of money and they were a little older than my classmates' parents which was weird but it was all I knew. My parents though, they were, let's just say that disapproving would be an understatement. I'm not blaming them but I need you to understand that when you grow up feeling as if you can never do anything right, it makes it difficult to trust other people. To trust that you're good enough, that you're worthy of their feelings."

Grady remained stone-faced and my confidence wavered.

"That probably explains a lot about my three failed marriages," I said and tried for a laugh that sounded more like an anguished squeak. "I already explained to you a little about Michael."

Finally he showed signs of life with a nod. "The ex who recently adopted twin girls."

I nodded. "Yes, that's him, but that's not really it. Michael was my best friend, probably the closest friend I ever had in the world. We shouldn't have gotten married, and we're both to blame for that mistake, but he didn't even have the decency to tell me he'd fallen in love with someone else, that I wasn't enough in our marriage until it was too late." My shoulders fell as that particular betrayal played in my mind all over again. "It was painful to hear him tell me all about the man he'd fallen in love with, and it obliterated my trust, Grady. If you can't trust that you're enough for your best friend or your parents, who can you trust?" My heart raced as the last of the words left my mouth, my mouth had gone dry as I waited for his response to the mess that was Margot.

Grady shook his head, and I couldn't tell if it was disgust or disappointment or something else entirely. He pinched the bridge of his nose for a long moment before he lifted his gaze to meet mine. "I don't know Margot, you could try trusting each person as they come into your life. I judged you based solely on your actions, not based on the other women from my past."

I nodded. "That's fair, and maybe if I was more balanced or had a healthy outlook on relationships, that's what I would have done. But years of putting up walls and barriers to keep people at a distance made it really difficult to stop doing that, even when I could see what I was doing and the consequences I would face if I didn't stop."

"So you're a product of your childhood and you can't change?" His tone hadn't thawed even a little, and a little more of my hope faded.

"We're all a product of our childhoods Grady, but no, that is certainly not what I'm saying. I'm just trying to make you understand that the scene at the bar wasn't really about me not trusting you, so much as my own insecurity. I didn't trust that I was enough for you. I saw a beautiful, young woman and assumed she was better than me and that you would think so too."

"I get that, I really do, but you have to understand that's not what it felt like to me."

"I know," I told him and took a step forward as I shook my head. "I shut off my emotions when it came to all personal relationships after Michael with just one goal, never to feel that sting of betrayal again. If I closed myself off and kept people at a distance then I wouldn't get hurt again."

"So shit talking my bar? Making feel beneath you?"

I flashed a sheepish grin and nodded. "Yep. If you hated me, then there was no risk of us ever becoming anything but enemies. And then my birthday happened."

"My birthday," he said with a small smile.

"Yes. On *our* birthday you were so nice to me and it took me off guard and forced me to admit the truth to myself. And then the incredible sex, I'll admit it scrambled my brain a little, which only made it easier to let you in, Grady."

"Sorry?"

I laughed. "And instead of being a jerk about the pregnancy, you were understanding and excited, it was too much to fight against, and I felt myself succumbing to your charms."

"And you were terrified," he guessed correctly.

I nodded. "I was worse than terrified Grady. You're gorgeous and entirely too young for me, and that combined with my own insecurities turned me into a version of myself I hardly recognized."

"Kind of an odd reaction to have for a man you think so little of," he grunted bitterly.

I resisted the urge to say something nasty in return and instead I just sighed and let the disappointment roll off my shoulders. "That's what I'm trying to tell you, if you'd remove that chip from your shoulder and just listen for once in your damn life!"

Grady's lips twitched with a grin. "I'm listening."

"I'm saying Grady that despite my best efforts and without me realizing it, I started to like you as a person. A man. That was alarming enough, but then that like turned into something more than like. Fondness or affection combined with attraction, I guess. And right now in this moment, I'm pretty sure that I'm in love with you." The last few words rushed out and I felt breathless. Exhausted.

He folded his thick arms across his wide chest and cocked a brow. "You're *pretty sure?*"

"Yes," I sighed. "I know it's not exactly the romantic declaration that you deserve, and it's silly at my age not to know your own heart for certain, but what I feel for you Grady is unlike anything I ever felt before. I thought I'd been in love before, a few times actually, but then you came along and turned all my ideas upside down."

Grady took a step forward and my heart soared again with hope. "So how do I make you feel Margot? Frustrated? Annoyed? Hot?"

"Yes to all of those, and so much more. I feel turned on with you, sure, but I feel safe in my attraction to you.

Confident that if I wanted to try something new you wouldn't make me feel bad about it. I feel amused and relaxed, like I can really and truly laugh without judgment. It's like I can be myself with you, which has given me the gift of learning who I really am when I'm not worried about the rest of the world. That is a heady and beautiful, and thoroughly horrifying feeling that I'm still getting used to, and it has made me behave badly, and for that Grady I'm sorry. I am really fucking sorry."

He grinned. "You said fuck."

"No," I said seriously. "I said *fucking*. There's a difference. Apparently." I lifted my chin high in the air, teasing and defiant.

"I liked it. Say it again," he demanded with the barest hint of a smile.

"No." That was all I said as my lips tugged into a teasing smile.

Grady stepped closer and closer still until we were toe to toe. "Say it."

My heart hitched at his nearness, the masculine scent of him and the intensity that burned in his blue eyes, not to mention the hope. Dear god, the hope had the power to undo me. "I'm not fucking saying it again Grady."

He grinned. "You will." One hand slid up the side of my face and his fingers tangled in my hair.

I shook my head as the rush of love and excitement ran through me, making me bold and confident. "Say what Grady? That I love you, or the word *fuck*."

He shrugged. "Either. Both."

I sucked in a deep breath, and when I released it the sound was shaky and breathless. This was it, the moment of truth, or rather the moment when I admitted the truth and risked my heart. Again.

"How about this? Grady, I *fucking* love you. I'm sure, and I'm scared, but I have a feeling that loving you is worth the risk of losing you."

"Good," he growled and hooked an arm around my waist so that my swollen belly and tender breasts were flush against his hard, strong body. "Because I fucking love you too, Margot. You drive me crazy in a million different ways, but there's no one I would rather fight or make up with than you babe."

My heart felt whole in that moment. Full and right and overwhelming, and Grady enhanced that feeling with a kiss so strong and powerful and intense that it stole my breath, my ability to think straight. I couldn't see or feel anything but this man and the strong beat of his heart, the possessive grip he had on me as he pulled me closer and devoured my mouth until I was nothing more than a puddle of need in his arms.

"Grady," I panted when he pulled back to stare at my face, to make certain this was what I wanted, that *he* was what I wanted. "I want this. I want you."

"Good, because I'm yours and you're mine." He scooped me in his arms and blew out the candles before he took us towards the staircase. "I got the better end of the deal," he growled and laid me across the bed.

Grady's intense gaze took in every single detail of my body, swollen and throbbing in the lingerie I'd chosen to entice him to listen. He kicked off his shoes and removed his shirt, then his pants until he was in just his dark green boxer briefs that hugged his thighs magnificently. "Margot," he growled and covered my body with his, loving on me until the wee hours of the morning.

It was more than I had hoped and dreamed for.

EPILOGUE

Margot & Grady ~ December

"Babe you look beautiful. Stop worrying, you're the guest of honor after all." I kissed Margot's neck as she frowned at her reflection in the mirror and wrapped my arms around her so my hands could cup her belly.

"Look at me Grady. I am about one thousand pounds, and I can't even get a pair of heels on my swollen feet and now this dress looks like a black velvet potato sack."

I smiled sweetly because the past few months have taught me that it's best not to argue with my pregnant, hormonal woman, and just get her what she needed.

"Hold that thought."

"Don't run away Grady! You did this to me, so you stay and you face the consequences."

I laughed loudly and rushed down the hall to the now

empty guest room, because after she told me she loved me, she moved into my bedroom—our bedroom—and she'd been there ever since. When I returned to the bedroom I stopped dead in my tracks at the sight of tears in her eyes. "I got you something."

She looked up through her watery gaze and sighed. "Please tell me you didn't buy me lingerie Grady. I can't take the disappointment." Her shoulders fell dejectedly as she maneuvered her way down onto the bed, and I went to her and laid the garment bag beside her.

"I'd like to think I'm a lot smarter than that. Open it up and decide for yourself." I pressed a kiss to her forehead and stepped back before I left her alone in the room to get dressed. I made my way downstairs where Carlotta and Mama worked on last-minute details for the baby shower. "Ladies. Need any help?"

Mama shooed me away. "No thanks. Your only job is to get Margot down here on time to greet the guests."

"And to make her feel beautiful," Carlotta added as she breezed into the living room in a green and white polka dot dress.

"Already did that. Where's Lance?"

Carlotta lit up when I mentioned the name of the little boy she and Chase had adopted when they eloped to Nashville and found the little boy eating their honeymoon leftovers. "He's at home with Chase, having a boys' day," she said and rolled her eyes, but even that could hide the affection she felt for them both.

"Savor it honey, because as soon as he gets here all he'll want is his mama. Boys," Mama huffed and shook her head as she looked at me. "You look handsome Grady."

"This old thing," I joked and opened the blue blazer Margot insisted went perfect with my eyes. I paired it with jeans and expensive sneakers, since this wasn't *just* a baby shower, because this was Margot Devereaux-Blanchard we were talking about.

Mama shook her head. "Who ever heard of a baby shower and dinner party? I don't know, but you sure clean up well boy."

I laughed. "It's Margot, Mama. She's always gotta have a little class with everything she does." And I loved that about her, the way she managed to make even small things feel like big, fancy events.

The doorbell rang, and needing to feel useful, I headed towards the door.

"Grady!" Margot's voice was loud and I couldn't quite figure out if that was shock or anger or something worse.

Mama shooed me towards the stairs. "It's probably Beth, I'll get it."

I nodded and slowly made my way upstairs, hoping this party wouldn't start with tears. Or shouts.

∽

I STARED at my reflection for what felt like an eternity after I yelled for Grady, uncertain how I felt. No, that's not true,

I felt beautiful and sexy, two things I thought were off the table until the babies were born and I shed my excess baby weight.

Leave it to Grady. I smiled and slipped on the comfy velvet flats I found at the bottom of the garment bag, eager to give Grady the first look.

He stopped halfway up the stairs and gulped. "Margot, holy hell woman that's a lot of cleavage." His gaze heated and he licked his lips.

I put a hand on my hip and rolled my eyes. "Apparently my stylist is a breast man."

He grinned. "Nothing wrong with a great pair of tits, babe. In that dress, yours are spectacular."

I flushed at his compliment and took one slow step towards him and then another. And another. "I love the dress. Thank you."

His gaze lasered in on my cleavage as he took my hand and kissed my forehead before he led me down the steps. "You look beautiful, purple is definitely your color."

"Purple velvet in December, who would have thought?"

"Me," he said proudly. "The best baby daddy stylist in all of Carson Creek."

"Damn Margot, you look hot!" Grady's sister Beth's words floated over all the commotion of guests arriving to celebrate the impending arrival of our twins, Marlo and Devlin.

All eyes turned to me and I froze until Grady squeezed

my hand and leaned in to whisper. "They're all stunned at how stunning you make pregnancy look."

I turned to him and smiled. "Have I told you how much I love you today?"

He shrugged and guided me down the rest of the stairs with a protective hand on my back. "I never get tired of hearin' it."

Or saying it. Every day he told me or showed me how he felt about me, and I no longer doubted him or us. We were strong on our own, and stronger together. "I love you Grady. So much."

He wiggled his brows. "I love it when you love me with that dirty mouth, babe." He took my hand and flung me to the wolves, also known as our friends and family, who had shown up for my nontraditional baby shower and dinner party.

"Can I touch your belly Miss Margot?"

I looked down into the jade green eyes of Carlotta's adopted son Lance. "Why?"

"I wanna feel the babies moving around in there. The babies *are* in there right?" He asked with all the innocence and curiosity of a seven year old.

I nodded. "Come here." I took his little hand and put on my belly to the twin's favorite spot. "Say hello."

"Hey there babies," he said in his thick Tennessee twang. "Holy moly!" Lance jumped back with a gasp when he received a solid kick. "Did that hurt?"

"No it just feels weird." I wasn't sure if I'd ever not be

in awe at the feeling of my babies moving around inside my body, and my time was almost up.

"All right Lance, let's give the other guests a chance to chat with Miss Margot." Chase grabbed the boy by the hand and led him towards the table stacked with appetizers. "I heard there was chocolate covered popcorn over there." And that was all it took to lure Lance away.

∼

"RYAN, GLAD YOU COULD MAKE IT." He'd been on tour with The Gregory Brothers for most of the fall, and Pippa and Ryanna had spent a lot of that time here at the house with Margot.

"Missed my girls," he said as he took in Pippa and Margot chatting and smiling, both unconscious rubbing pregnant bellies. "And Margot's dinner parties are not to be missed. You guys went all out."

I shrugged at his words. "It's a big deal. Our first babies, and more so because she thought this would never happen for her."

He sighed and looked at his wife with love in his eyes. "Trust me when I tell you it's always a big deal. Baby number two feels as exciting as baby number one, just less scary."

"Is that why you're back mid-tour?"

"Yeah. This is our last tour for a while, so Roman can focus on his solo gig and Derek can focus on producing, which means I get to spend more time here at home. Plus they extended the tour, and we demanded to have a few weeks off before the holiday gigs."

"Pippa said they were gonna join you on tour?"

Ryan nodded. "They're supposed to, but this pregnancy isn't as easy as the first, so we'll see."

"Sounds like you could use a beer," I told him and nodded towards the kitchen.

Ryan's brows shot up. "Margot lets you keep beer in this joint?"

I scowled. "This is my house too," I told him with a grin. "Plus, my woman has excellent taste and signed me up for one of those craft brewery subscriptions. You'll see."

Gathered around the beer fridge was Trey, Roman and Derek. "This is unreal," Derek sighed in awe. "You better marry that woman and soon."

I didn't say so, but I fully planned to. "Right?"

"If you don't, I will," Roman said and pulled a red ale from the fridge and lifted it in the air. "She's wearing pregnancy well. Very well," he purred.

"I'd hate for you to go back on tour with a black eye," I told him only half-joking.

Roman grinned. "It'll only make the chicks want me more."

"Will you guys be here for the wedding?" Trey asked the question because he and Valona had planned a small Christmas Eve wedding with only a few close friends and their three girls.

Derek shrugged. "Allegedly, but the tour is selling so well they keep adding dates. Bella's already got her dress, and a little birdie told me that Everest's tie and pocket square matches Keri's dress."

The group fell silent and all eyes turned to see Trey's reaction. Trey smiled and shrugged. "Who do you think had to call the dress shop to not only get the exact color, but a fabric sample to give to your woman?"

A round of masculine laughter erupted around the beer fridge and we all grabbed something before joining our women in the living room.

～

"Lacey! I wasn't sure you guys were going to be able to make it!" Lacey and Levi showed up just before the shower officially began with Mikey standing between them. The adorable little boy had become fast friends with Lance and made a beeline for him as soon as he spotted him.

Lacey smiled and wrapped me in a hug. "We weren't sure either but we leave tomorrow for Cambodia to cover the coup attempt and I wanted to make sure we dropped off a gift for the little ones. They'll probably be here before we get back."

"Let's hope so? Or hope not," I shrugged, not really sure.

Levi laughed and enveloped me in a hug. "I hope your babies stay put until they're good and ready, as for

Cambodia I'm not sure what I'm hoping for yet. Kind of looking forward to an adventure like this with Lacey."

"Sounds like you two have something up your sleeve. Want to share?"

Lacey and Levi wore matching grins and shook their head simultaneously. "Nothing to tell," Lacey assured me. "At least nothing that I'm aware of."

"I don't believe you. Either of you."

Levi shook his head. "That's because you're a suspicious woman," he flashed a teasing grin. "But I do have some news," he said and held up a copy of the Carson Creek Daily Journal.

I grabbed the paper and opened it up with a gasp at the full page ad just as Carlotta called for the guests to gather for the gift opening portion of the celebration.

The smaller groups all converged on the spacious living with the cozy furniture that was the perfect place for a baby shower. I took my seat on the plush lounge Grady insisted on buying so I could get work done away from the office in my current state.

Carlotta stood in the middle of the room with her hands clasped together. "Before we start with the gifts, Grady has something he'd like to say."

Grady stepped forward, a big an imposing figure even in the middle of a crowd. He smiled at everyone and winked at me. "It looks as if we have more to celebrate than the arrival of Marlo and Devlin and I'm hoping to add more one thing to the list." He flashed a nervous grin and turned to face me. "Margot, babe. We have had quite the road to get here, haven't we? Enemies first and then friends, then loves and finally, family."

I blinked away tears that started to form because I didn't want to miss one moment of whatever beautiful words he spoke next.

"Once we stopped fightin' the inevitable, we created something really special together."

"Very special," I agreed with a shaky breath.

His shoulders sagged with relief. "We fell in love and every day for months we've lived out our version of happily ever after. With the twins comin' soon, the picture will be complete. Almost." He came to me and knelt down at my side. "I know you want the fairytale babe and I want to be the man to give it to you, starting with this." Grady produced a gorgeous cushion cut diamond that was pale pink in color, surrounded by dozens of smaller white diamonds. "Margot Devereaux-Blanchard, love of my life, mother of my twins and classiest woman I have ever met, will you do me the honor of marrying me and livin' out our happy ending for the rest of our lives?"

I blinked and nodded, unable to find my words at his heartfelt words and unexpected proposal. "Grady, you're sure?"

"Positive. You're mine already babe and I can't wait to see you float down the aisle or the meadow in a big white dress. What do you say?"

"I say hell yes! I love you." I tried in vain to slide to the edge of the lounger to get my hands on my man but I failed and Grady wrapped his arms around me and held me tight, kissed me long and hard.

"I love you too Margot." The love shone in his eyes and I couldn't look away as he slid the ring on my finger and brushed a kiss to the back of my hand. "So damn much."

I let out a shaky breath at his growled words and pressed my forehead to his. "Right back at you Grady. Forever."

"Hey man, you stole my thunder!" Derek joked from his spot beside Bella on the sofa.

I laughed and shook my head. "Congratulations on your engagement I told the happy couple. Levi just showed me the announcement."

Bella shook her head. "He couldn't resist a full page ad announcing our engagement. Congratulations to you too."

Grady stood and smiled at Derek. "Let's see who gets down the aisle first."

"After the babies," I said over their macho posturing.

"After the tour," Bella added. "But before the baby." The room fell silent for a long moment and then erupted in applause and whistles and words of congratulations.

I leaned back in the lounge and looked at all the people who had gathered to celebrate with me and Grady today. These were my friends, they were my family. They were my tribe. No, they were *our* tribe.

All this time I'd been trying to run away from love, to keep people at a distance and it turned out I had a whole community right here who loved me and wanted the best for me.

And now I had it all.

Everything I ever wanted.

"Love you," Grady mouthed the words to me and winked.

No I had so much more than I wanted and it all started with a drunken birthday celebration with a sexy tattooed bartender.

∼

Check out the other books in the Midlife Series.

PREVIEW: CURVY NANNY FOR THE GRUMPY SINGLE DAD

A **Curvy Nanny** meets a **Grumpy Billionaire Single Dad** in this **Forced Proximity** romance.

Nanny Rule #1: *Don't fall for the Daddy.*

No one likes an entitled pr*ck who cuts people off in traffic with his flashy car.

Not even when he looks like sex on wheels with dreamy dark hair and piercing green eyes.

And especially not when he turns out to be the single father of my new charge.

Dante Rush is beautiful, grumpy and oh so annoying.

It'll take all of my experience as a nanny to make it through this job without throttling the handsome jerk.

Then one moonlit kiss and I can barely remember my name, never mind my rules for staying professional.

One kiss turned into another and then another, and suddenly,

I'm in love with my boss.

Losing my heart to the grumpy billionaire is bad enough.

But I can't afford to lose my job too.

CHAPTER 1
LUCY

"Where's Daddy?"

I couldn't ignore Lena's worried tone over her father's absence even if I wanted to, because those big blue eyes damn near broke my heart.

I glanced at the clock again. It was after nine and Dante still wasn't home, which was unlike him, and worse, he hadn't called. In fact he hadn't called all day which I'd arrogantly believed was because he finally trusted me to do my job. But now I couldn't deny the fact that something was very likely seriously wrong.

"I'm not sure Lena."

"He always says good night," she whined and her lip quivered.

He didn't just say good night. Dante usually tucked her, read her a story before he kissed her good night and wished her sweet dreams. *Think fast, Lucy.* I had to come up with something before tears or a tantrum came, neither of which were good around bed time.

"I have an idea!"night

"Call Daddy?"

That would be the best idea, but if something had actually happened to him, I didn't want to hear the news with Lena watching and listening. "Better. We'll make a video of you telling him good night and that you love him, so he won't feel bad about missing out tonight. How does that sound?"

"Okay," she said around sniffles.

Relief coursed through me at her easy agreement and I pulled my phone out of my back pocket and set it down before I settled her in bed. "Let's get you under the blankets so he feels like he was right here with you."

"Okay!" She was such a sweet girl, so accepting of everything life had thrown her way, and somehow able to get excited about the smallest things. "How's this Lucy?" She smiled up at me with the blankets tucked up under her armpits.

"Perfect." I held up the phone and tapped the record button. "Okay, what do you want to tell Daddy?"

"Good night Daddy! I love you and I miss you, but don't miss bedtime again, okay? Love you, good night!" She collapsed back onto the bed and sighed. "Was that good?"

"He'll love it," I assured her and sat down on the bed.

"I know it's not the same, but I'm happy to read you a bedtime story, if you want?"

"Okay Lucy." Lena settled under her blankets and listened while I read a story about a ladybug who loved to make friends, but she quickly fell asleep. Dante typically made it home for dinner, so since about six this evening Lena had been worried about her father.

"Good night honey." I pressed a kiss to her forehead and sighed as I backed out of the room and turned off the light. I wasn't sure if Lena would sleep peacefully given how the past few hours had gone, so I grabbed my e-reader and curled up on one of the plush sofas in the sitting room.

I was so engrossed in the romance that I didn't hear the front door as it opened and then closed, or the sound of Dante's designer loafers on the floor until his shadow fell over me and my e-reader. His unexpected appearance startled a gasp out of me, but I recovered quickly and looked up with a frown.

"You look like hell." Handsome as hell to be sure, but also like he'd been to hell and back in the ten or so hours he'd been gone.

His scowl darkened. "You don't. What's your point?"

I resisted the urge to smile at his unintended compliment and instead took a long look at his beautiful face. "Rough day?"

Dante nodded and raked a hand through his thick hair as he blew out a long exhale that contained so many emotions that my heart went out to him. "It was a nightmare. Everything that could go wrong today did."

"You want dinner?"

His look only darkened at my question. "That's not your job."

"Duh," I rolled my eyes. "It's called basic human kindness. Look it up when you have a chance." I stood and put some distance between us by warming up the leftover dinner.

"I'm kind," he insisted, his voice closer behind me than I expected.

"If you say so Dante." I turned slowly, which was a mistake, because he was entirely too close, and all of my curves were brushing against him from the front, the counter at my back. "Excuse me."

He took a step closer and I held my breath. "You afraid of me Lucy?"

I laughed. "Hardly. It's just called personal space." I sucked in a breath and skirted around him. "Why don't you go kiss Lena and get changed out of your work clothes?"

He frowned. "Are you a parenting expert now, on top of all your many other skills?"

I rolled my eyes and gave his chest a shove. "You're an ass, Mr. Rush. Lena was worried from the moment you didn't show up for dinner until I managed to get her to go to sleep. She thought something happened to you."

"She knows I would never leave her." He let out an

exaggerated scoff just to make sure I knew what he thought about my words.

"Okay fine." I pulled out my phone and sent him the video. "Do what you want, I'm going to bed." I boiled with frustration, so I turned around, ready to grab my e-reader and turn in for the night.

"Lucy," he growled and grabbed my arm to stop me from walking away.

"Let me go, Dante."

"I'm sorry," he growled. "It's been a long day and I'm exhausted."

I shrugged out of his hold and sighed. "All the more reason to go see Lena." I took a step forward and he pulled me back close, but not quite flush against his broad chest. Our gazes collided, his angry and mine shocked. Deep breaths rushed out of us both, and Dante looked as if he wanted to say something, probably scathing to me. In the end, he released me and left the kitchen, stalking up the stairs to his daughter's room.

I let myself have a satisfied smile and rolled my eyes over the stubborn man. He was contrary sometimes just to be contrary, and it was very frustrating, luckily he wasn't my charge. Still, I knew what it was like to have a long hellish day, so I re-heated his dinner before I returned to the living room to retrieve my e-reader once again.

"Stay," Dante ordered as he jogged down the stairs a few minutes later in a fresh pair of lounge pants and a t-shirt that molded perfectly to his chest and arms.

"I am not a dog," I grunted and set my e-reader aside.

He stopped halfway between the bottom of the stairs and the kitchen, his shoulders fell forward and he sighed. "Please stay."

Indecision warred within me. Part of me wanted to run up the stairs before he returned from the kitchen, just because I could, but that would be petty. Hilarious, but petty.

"Thanks for dinner." Dante returned and dropped down on the sofa, leaving one cushion between us as he kicked his legs up on the coffee table. "It's delicious."

I shrugged and tugged my legs up to my chest. "Don't thank me, Dotty is the one who made it."

"You warmed it up," he insisted with a panty melting smile.

"Job security." I kept my expression blank as a slow smile crossed his face.

"Liar."

I shrugged again and met his smile with one of my own. "You'll never know."

"Thank you for the video. It was sweet and just what I needed." He dug into the food, eating it as if he hadn't enjoyed a meal in weeks. "Even in her sleep, Lena clung to me."

I nodded to acknowledge that I was listening, but I hated that I felt my heart softening towards this stubborn man. Why was it so damn attractive that he loved his kid? He was a father, he was supposed to love and care for his child, and no man should get extra points for doing what mothers have been doing for thousands of years.

"You should call if you're going to be late. I know it's not always convenient, but it would make Lena worry less."

Dante's nostrils flared angrily and I wasn't even surprised. The man couldn't take any type of criticism. It probably made him a beast of a boss. Then he surprised me by saying nothing, he just returned to his food without a word.

"You know Dante, not every drop of advice is a criticism. It's merely a suggestion, to let Lena be a little girl instead of a ball of anxiety."

His jaw clenched again, but I was undeterred.

"She's already lost her mother, and if you could have seen her worry tonight you would understand my concern."

"Stop!" He barked. "Just...stop Lucy."

My mouth snapped shut and my eyes widened at his tone, or more accurately, my response to his commanding tone. It was hot and forceful, which I apparently liked. "You know, I think I will stop. Good night, Dante." I stood, and this time I didn't take my time, I just grabbed my e-reader and hit the stairs.

"Lucy..." he called after me, but I kept moving, refusing to be derailed by the infernal man. "Dammit."

I couldn't help but smile to myself, that for once in his life Dante wouldn't get his way. Not with me.

"Lucy," he growled again, but this time his hand snaked out and gripped my upper arm.

Where in the hell had he come from? "Didn't anyone ever tell you to keep your hands to yourself, Mr. Rush?"

When he spun me to face him, heat flared in Dante's eyes and I couldn't look away. My heart raced and my breath caught in my throat. "You annoy the hell out of me, woman."

"I feel the same way about you."

He let out a low grunt and then his lips were on mine, his mouth devoured me hungrily, and when his arms wrapped around me to pull me closer, I held on tight. The kiss was hot as fuck, too hot for someone I actively disliked, but damn, he kissed like a dream. His hands slipped from my shoulders down to my waist before he cupped my ass and brought me flush against an impressive length of hardness.

I moaned into his mouth, and his tongue slipped inside. Dante deepened the kiss and stoked the fire that burned through my veins. The kiss was like a revelation, like I hadn't been truly kissed until this moment, which was pretty disconcerting. Still, as much as I told my brain to pull back, to stop this magical nonsense, I couldn't do it. He tasted too good.

Felt too good.

My hands gripped his shoulder and I told myself to use his strength to push away, to end this erotic torture before I did something crazy, like beg him to strip me down and make me scream his name. It was madness and I was powerless to stop it. I leaned into it, devoured his mouth the way he did mine until I was dizzy and horny and out of my mind with lust.

The kiss was eternal, but that was the type of dangerous thinking that I couldn't afford, so finally I managed to slowly pull back, my gaze unfocused and my lips swollen.

"Lucy," he moaned and his fingertips dug into my flesh.

He's your boss. Dammit. I stepped back until his hands fell away, my eyes wide with shock. This was exactly what he expected of me, and all women in fact.

Shit, shit, shit. I took one step back and then another and another until I felt the doorknob of my bedroom pressed against the small of my back. I turned it quickly and stepped in. "I should, ah, get to bed. Early day," I said by way of a totally unbelievable explanation.

"Right," he said shakily. "See you tomorrow."

I nodded absently, slammed the door and pressed my back against it. I kissed my boss. Well, more accurately he kissed me and I did nothing to stop it, which to his warped mind, probably meant that I was trying to find my way into his bed.

Stupid, stupid girl.

I spent most of the night reliving the hottest kiss I'd ever experienced and worrying that Dante would use it as an excuse to get rid of me.

DEAR READER,

Thank you for taking the time to read this excerpt. I hope you enjoyed it,

If you'd like to read more of **Curvy Nanny for the Grumpy Single Dad**, please scan the QR code below.

Piper

Also by Piper Sullivan

Nanny Series

Curvy Nanny for the Nerd

Curvy Fake Wife for the Player

Curvy Nanny for the Grumpy Single Dad

Small Town Lovers

Midlife Baby: Morgot & Grady

Midlife Fake Out: Bella & Derek

Midlife Love Affair: Lacy & Levi

Midlife Valentine: Valona & Trey

Midlife Do Over: Pippa & Ryan

Healing Love

Dueling Drs, Book 6: Zola & Drew

Rockstar Baby Daddy, Book 5: Susie & Gavin

Unfriending the Dr, Book 4: Persy & Ryan
Kissing the Dr, Book 3: Megan & Casey
Loving the Nurse, Book 2: Gus & Antonio
Falling for the Dr, Book 1: Teddy & Cal

Curvy Girl Dating Agency

Forever Curves, Book 8: Brenna & Grant
Small Town Curves, Book 7: Shannon & Miles
Curvy Valentine Match, Book 6: Mara & Xander
Misbehaving Curves, Book 5: Joss & Ben
Curves for the Single Dad, Book 4: Tara & Chris
His Curvy Best Friend, Book 3: Sophie & Stone
Curvy Girl's Secret, Book 2: Olive & Liam
His Curvy Enemy, Book 1: Eva & Oliver

Small Town Protectors (Tulip Series)

That Hot Night, Book 12: Janey & Rafe
To Catch A Player, Book 11: Reece & Jackson
Cold Hearted Love, Book 10: Ginger & Tyson
Hero Boss, Book 9: Stevie & Scott
Dr's Orders, Book 8: Maxine & Derek
Mastering Her Curves, Book 7: Mikki & Nate
Kissing My Best Friend, Book 6: Bo & Jase

Undesired, Book 5: Hope & Will

Wanting Ms Wrong, Book 4: Audrey & Walker

Loving My Enemy, Book 3: Elka & Antonio

Bad Boy Benefits, Book 2: Penny & Ry

Hero In My Bed, Book 1: Nina & Preston

Accidental Hookups

Accidentally Hitched, Book 1: Viviana & Nash

Accidentally Wed, Book 2: Maddie & Zeke

Accidentally Bound, Book 3: Trish & Mason

Accidentally Wifed, Book 4: Magenta & Davis

Boardroom Games

His Takeover: An Enemies to Lovers Romance (Boardroom Games Book 1)

Sinful Takeover: An Enemies to Lovers Romance (Boardroom Games Book 2)

Naughty Takeover: An Enemies to Lovers Romance (Boardroom Games 3)

Boxsets & Collections

Small Town Misters: A Small Town Protectors Boxset

Misters of Pleasure: A Small Town Protectors Boxset

Misters of Love: A Small Town Romance Boxset

Misters of Passion: A Small Town Romance Boxset

Kiss Me, Love Me: An Alpha Male Romance Boxset

Accidentally On Purpose: A Marriage Mistake Boxset

Daddies & Nannies: A Contemporary Romance Boxset

Cowboys & Bosses: A Contemporary Romance Boxset

About the Author

Piper Sullivan is an old school romantic who enjoys reading romantic stories as much as she enjoys writing them.

She spends her time day-dreaming of dashing heroes and the feisty women they love.

Visit Piper's website www.pipersullivan.com

Join Piper's Newsletter for quirky commentary, new romance releases, freebies and contests.

Check her out on BookBub

Stalk her on Facebook

Printed in Dunstable, United Kingdom